Edited by Douglas Glover

Best Canadian Stories
05

We acknowledge the support of the Canada Council for the Arts, the Government of Ontario through the Ontario Media Development Corporation and the Government of Canada through the Book Publishing Industry Development-ment Program for our publishing activities.

"Across Some Dark Avenue of Plot He Carried Her Body" by Elisabeth Harvor and "The Riddles of Aramaic" by Elise Levine were first published in *The Malahat Review*; "A Matter of Firsts" by Krista Bridge originally appeared in *Descant*; "Roppongi Story" by David Whitton and "Most Wanted" by Vivette J. Kady first appeared in *The New Quarterly*.

The following magazines were consulted: *Capilano Review, Descant, Event, Fiddlehead, Geist, Grain, Malahat Review, Matrix, New Orphic Review, New Quarterly, The New Yorker, Prairie Fire, Prism international, Quarry, Saturday Night, Toro* and *Toronto Life*.

ISBN 0 7780 1269 7 (hardcover)
ISBN 0 7780 1270 0 (softcover)
ISSN 0703 9476

Cover art by Simon Battensby/Masterfile
Book design by Michael Macklem

Printed in Canada

PUBLISHED IN CANADA BY OBERON PRESS

Contributions for the thirty-sixth volume, published or unpublished, should be sent to Oberon Press, 205—145 Spruce Street, Ottawa, Ontario KIR 6PI before 31 March, 2006. All manuscripts should enclose a stamped self-addressed envelope.

David Helwig's "Stitches in Air" is a demon-lover story shadowed by death, regret and bitter experience, the kind of story a writer begins to write with the wisdom of years at his elbow, with the knowledge that time eats her children. Helwig is a member of Can Lit's old guard, one of half-a-dozen writers in this country who can regularly turn out stories that are brilliant, thick with detail, plot twist and resonance, almost casual in their technical mastery. In this case, watch especially the lovely pattern he makes with lace, lace-making and surgical sutures (a doctor stitches up his lover's wound).

The remaining stories this year are, yes, similarly dark, dangerous and masterful even when they're written by the new guard. In Darryl Whetter's "The Organic Milk Rapist" a savagely comic illicit role-playing love-affair veers magically toward a happy, domestic ending. Krista Bridge's "A Matter of Firsts" is the tale of a thirteen-year-old girl who meets and befriends her father's mistress only to witness the fading of his cynical enthusiasm. He gets to say the cruelest brush-off line I've ever read: "There are experiences diminished by companionship." Elise Levine's "The Riddles of Aramaic" is the story of a young, running-obsessed grief counsellor who can't connect with her dying clients; her failure of empathy is the flipside of her inability to see her own death waiting in the wings.

In "Most Wanted" Vivette J. Kady tells the story of a guitarist who gets electrocuted by his amp, the wife who leaves him to join a Christian commune, and Duane, the three-legged dog he buys for company. "Weird," says the wife, "how you and Duane have this affliction." In Michael Bryson's elliptical, dialogue-driven story "Six Million Million Miles" we read about a suddenly middle-aged man discovering that his latest lover has discarded him when she brings another man for drinks. In Kim Aubrey's "A Large Dark" a recently divorced father tries to find a date in a evening painting-class,

7

struggles to keep house with a slovenly but good-hearted nanny, and lives in fear that his wife will steal his son.

Elisabeth Harvor contributes a story called "Across Some Dark Avenue of Plot He Carried Her Body" which is as much about love and the art of story-writing as it is about a lonely Montreal creative-writing teacher who fends off power-plays by theory-mad poets, fights for privacy against her menacing apartment super, and nearly dies of asphyxiation due to a faulty generator during the great ice-storm of 1997 (she's saved by a gentle fireman). In the end she thinks, "I also saw that whether you're a firefighter or a writer, there's a deep but fleeting tenderness you can offer to those who need to be saved or remembered."

And in "Roppongi Story" David Whitton writes about a man who runs away from a job and marriage (marriage goes bad and he sleeps with his wife's sister) and tries to lose himself in Japan only to discover friendship and wisdom in the guise of a very drunken Japanese businessman named Mr. Taguchi, who sums up the meaning of life in deliriously fractured English: "This area are very, very superb and also very peculiar, full of wretched sorrow and beautiful splendour. Is difficult to wonder."

DOUGLAS GLOVER

Across Some Dark Avenue of Plot He Carried Her Body

Elisabeth Harvor

Back in the days when I was still teaching at Stanopolis College, I had one good class and one bad class. Or the classes would alternate, change places like dancers. Teaching filled me with fear on those long fall and winter afternoons. I was a child again, a child in a schoolyard who knows who the bullies are and tries to steer clear of them. But now the bullies were militant theorists who were twenty years younger than I was and two times a week we were all trapped together in the same windowless classroom. To outwit them—and also to head off the kinds of discussion that would lead us into the banal territory of sociology or the deranged territory of critical theory—I brought assignments to my classes:

1. This is a "free writing" exercise, and you will have exactly three minutes to complete it. Begin writing when I say GO, and don't stop until I say STOP. Make a narrative out of the following words: snow, blur, coffee, hood, sad, windy, yellow. Don't edit your work. And don't stop to think.
2. Translate the following paragraph of Portuguese into English. Don't be concerned if you can't read Portuguese. The point of the exercise is to free associate to the look of the words on the page, then make your own inspired translations.

While my students were writing, I would sit at my end of the seminar table and try to catch up on marking their work, and one October afternoon when I was writing a note warning a student poet not to abandon the weeds and bolts that he tended to make such good use of in his poems for the flashier seductions of

9

"the phantoms, the mad hounds, the friends and foes, and other horrors," I could barely concentrate, I was so wild with worry that my landlord, Guido Gallo—a man who was the maddest of mad hounds in real life—had let himself into my apartment and was doing God knows what there: spitting his vile spit into the bowls of pesto and scallopine al Marsala in my refrigerator, going through the bank statements in the central drawer of my desk, searching among my panties and slips for whatever evidence he could find of the depraved sexual life I didn't even have. But I couldn't move out, my apartment floated among the tops of the hazy green trees and my rent was too low. The other women tenants were afraid of him too. We all knew that three times a week he went off to karate classes and that he was rumoured to be on steroids, extra testosterone.

My most difficult student at Stanopolis that year was Norval Tapp-Hansen, a very tall sociology transfer who had long white hair and a mournful look. Back in September he had nearly started a mutiny in my bad class when he'd made a power grab for control of it and he still had a following among three of the male students. But in spite of his extraordinary height and physical charisma, he seemed an odd candidate for leader or alpha male, he was too knock-kneed and fidgety. And he talked too much. On the first day of class, he chose the chair at the Papa end of the table and, as the weeks wore on, no other student dared to sit in this chair, not even on the days that Norval Tapp-Hansen didn't come to class. So that even when he wasn't at school, he was present. Or as he himself might have put it, he was "delivering absence as presence."

The fall semester came to an end on the tenth of December. We took our break late and when we came back to the seminar-room we had nothing left to critique but Norval's most recent poem. I asked him to read it aloud and we all sat with our eyes fixed on it as he read to us:

LIFE'S LONG GOODBYE AND
THE LAST SPLICED HELLO

Or songs, the sea's blue drift & it's open
Door to the roar, its sincopated tumble

Down the stairs in the dark
Night of the Impetuous

O estuary! O regalia!

Prehistoric vamoose, frayed darkness,
Life's long goodbye & the last spliced hello

To the circumspect instruments
Limp as Dali's watches & limp as our own

Ho-hum and dumb dumb appendages

How can I walk when my poor heart is thus injured,
O destroyed & maimed heart, why dust thou limp?

As I looked up for help, my students looked down. I would have to be the one to begin then, and since we always tried to make our first comments positive, I began by telling Norval that I liked the frayed darkness and the dark night of the impetuous, then I spoke of how the poem began in *medias res* and went on to say that the final line of the poem, "A line in which the Fool, perhaps, is speaking, is almost Shakespearean, the spelling of 'dost' as 'dust' being either inspired or an accident...."

Norval stared at me. He wasn't committing himself.

"This is also quite a bit more coherent than your usual work...."

The other students all laughed at this.

"But although you've used a number of improbable and inventive phrases and word fragments," I said, "I do also need to draw your attention to several spelling errors and grammatical confusions. For example, do you mean the *it's* in 'it's open door' to be a possessive? Or do you mean it to be a contraction?"

"It's a contraction in the sense that it has made a contract with rhythm," Norval said.

"How so?"

"Rhythm is such a contrary word," he said. "It has so many consonants and only one vowel."

I asked him where the vowel was.

"Oh, well, the 'e' is silent."

"It's also invisible."

"Rhythm should be spelled 'mimi,'" he said.

"But the problem *is*," I said, holding out one hand as if I were about to sprinkle a shirt so I could iron it, "you are sprinkling your lines with commas and apostrophes at random." And I got up from my chair, reminding myself that I should get up from my chair more often and do something physical, theatrical, so that when the Evaluation forms were handed out at the end of the term, my students would remember my going to the blackboard and consequently conclude that they must have learned something. I printed MY, YOUR, HIS, HER, THEIR, WHOSE, ITS, ADAM'S in one column. Then after I'd read each word aloud, I added the word "apple" to it. When I called out "Adam's apple," everyone laughed. "I want you to print ADAM'S APPLE in capital letters at the top of this list," I told them. Then I printed THAT'S, WHO'S, WHAT'S, WHERE'S, HOW'S, WHEN'S, WHY'S, IT'S in another column. "And I want you to print THAT IS AND WHO IS AND IT IS at the top of *this* list. I moved the pointer back to the first list. "What are these words called?"

"Possessives!" three or four voices called out.

"And if a woman's baby is pushing its way out into the world, what are her labour pains called?"

The women in the class shouted with one massed shout, like cheerleaders: "Contractions!"

I moved the pointer over to my second list. "And these words are called what?"

"Contractions!"

I drew a circle around the ITS. "Rebecca, could you please compose a sentence using this word?"

"Her baby is pushing its way out into the world," Rebecca said in a weary voice, as if she found it distasteful that there were still people in this class who were unable to make these necessary distinctions. She had hazy black hair that was given variety here and there by a skinny black braid that appeared to have been oiled, then brightened by trinkets that looked more like aluminum than silver and she was the only one of my students who really knew the rules of grammar. I wondered if she had gone to a private school instead of to one of the huge Montreal high schools. I even wondered if she had attended la crème de la crème of schools for girls in Montreal, Miss Edgar's and Miss Cramp's.

"Excellent," I said. Then I glanced over at Vince, a student who was a secret favourite of mine. I pointed at the IT'S. "Vince, could you please compose a sentence using this word?"

"It's the end of the civilized world as we know it."

"Also excellent."

Vince looked like an unhealthy football player, or some sort of unhealthy athlete, an athlete on a bad cafeteria diet, but he was a wonderful writer. "Toward the bottom of the poem," he now said, looking up at Norval, "the words 'limp as our own ho-hum and dumb dumb appendages' intrigue me. Are they meant to suggest that the poem is about sexual impotence? Or impotence in general, perhaps? Perhaps even artistic impotence?"

"It's not *about* any single or particular thing," said Norval.

No, I thought, of course not, and after another ten minutes of class discussion about what the poem might mean, I asked Norval if the *dumb* of 'dumb dumb appendages' meant dumb as in not very intelligent. "Or does it mean dumb as in speechless?"

"Both. One dumb is for not very intelligent, the other dumb is for speechless."

But of course, I thought, why even ask, *mah appendage is speechless, man*, and as I walked down the length of the table to hand out the pages of a new assignment, I could hear the buzz and rustling of whispers all around me and I wondered if my other students were coming to the same conclusion.

Once everyone was beginning to write, I sat at my end of the table again and began to leaf through the booklet containing the course lists for the spring semester. I had to marvel as I stealthily turned its pages, the university secretaries must have been having such a bad day the afternoon they typed up the lists. There was a course offering an 'in-depth look at the working relationship of Leonard Woof and Virginia Woof. Reading list: Leonard Woof: *Stories from the East* and the autobiography, as well as excerpts from the political writing; Virginia Woof: *To* the *Lighthouse, Mrs. Dalloway,* and *The Waves.*' I tried to recall the name of Virginia Woolf's dog since Woolf's writing about him would, I thought, make a fine addition to the list.

"You can hand your work in as you leave," I told my students, and on their way out of class they did, although a few of them lingered at the door to thank me. Lionel, who wore his hair in blue spikes, his single gold hoop of an earring threaded through a tiny skull of ivory plastic, joined them. "Hey, Gina!" he called over to me. "Merry merry whatever!" I felt affection for him, even though he wasn't as good a writer as the others, his poems were too noble and wispy.

Only Norval Tapp-Hansen stayed behind after the others had gone. He came up to my end of the table and stood breathing beside me as I was forcing papers into my briefcase. I felt tense having him so near, he had read so much more critical theory than I had. But what did this, in the end, matter? He was a parrot. He was a parrot who was asking me if he could have a few words with me.

My heart sank. "Of course," I told him. "Walk with me. I have to walk over to the library at Concordia."

As we came blinking out into the dull December afternoon, he was already telling me that part of his struggle this year, as always, was to try to overcome his cynicism.

I took this to be a criticism of my teaching methods, but I let it pass. It bothered me, though, that he could speak in such an upholstered voice and still hope to pass himself off as a rebel. The words he chose bothered me, too: "thus" and "therefore" and "they exist as an effect of a specific linguistic, if you will, structure."

If you will.

As the late afternoon traffic kept roaring past us, I couldn't help but secretly smile at the thought of what an odd couple we must make, Norval the tall Dane or albino looming over me, a petite, nearsighted Canadian of Italian descent.

"Thus, if you have any preconceived or dogmatic commitment to one effect over another," Norval was saying, "play is only possible to an *extent.*"

"Agreed," I said. And only after too long a silence had the wit to add, "Obviously."

"In fact, my view is that anything is permissible insofar as it feeds into what the poem *says*," said Norval. "But that, of course, presumes that the poet wants to 'say' something. Most don't."

I was wanting to speak about a few poems that were out in the world that I thought were pretty damn good, but we were interrupted by the siren of an ambulance racing its whine past us on its way to the Royal Vic and it occurred to me that it might be amusing to invent a village called Insofar and locate it in the Outer Hebrides. Or in Iceland. But I also found myself thinking of Gallo again, much as I would have preferred not to. I saw him in my apartment once again, going from one room to another. He was horrible to everyone, but he seemed to reserve his most virulent hatred for me. I wondered if this was because he took me for some sort of ex-hippie (intricately patterned scarves, overgrown unruly dark hair, haphazardly patterned vests) when the women he approved were in all likelihood the sort of heavily perfumed women who wore aqua pantsuits along with squarish brassy earrings and chunky bracelets that clinked. Or anything, really, that was pastel and vulgar. But now he was back in my bedroom again and lifting a pair of plum silk panties out of my underwear drawer and deciding (merely because they were mine) that they were cut too low at the hips. Even so, he was placing them on the flowered bottom sheet of my unmade bed, then lowering his naked body down on top of them.

"…example of how I navigate in the world," Norval was saying.

I wanted to say to him, But my darling Norval, just who, exactly, do you think you *are*? Magellan?" But I knew he was only spouting the thrilling idiocies of the advanced poetry workshops led by one of my rivals, that he was only in love with its grandiloquent verbs.

"However, I do also like to use language in ways that are far more exciting than the simple games or figures of speech we've been using thus far in our workshop this year...."

Thus far, insofar, therefore, however.

A statuesque black woman was walking toward us. She was wearing a mauve mohair cape and long black gloves pulled up past her elbows, each of her wrists held in the clasp of a silver bracelet the width of a napkin ring, and she seemed to know exactly where she was going in this life. But by this time Gallo was standing in front of the bookcase next to my bed. I arranged for his glance to quickly pass by *The Story of O,* hoping he would mistake it for the sort of book parents buy to teach their children everything about a particular letter in the alphabet. As for *Lolita,* I hoped he might decide it was only a boring book about the summer camp adventures of an Italian girl.

"For example, using metonymy and puns as opposed to similes and metaphors...."

"Some puns can be quite amusing, true," I said, "but don't you also find them sort of obvious and predictable? And any headline writer for any newspaper or magazine can do them. Last week, for example, in a copy of *Vogue* that I happened to pick up at my dentist's, a perfume ad was headed SCENTS AND SENSIBILITY...."

"But that's really quite brilliant," he said.

I squinted up at him. "Whereas a metaphor is a kind of visual *code*," I said, noting that I too was beginning to speak in italics. "An inspired comparison that honours or *celebrates*, often even with *cruelty*, some artifact or person or animal or smile or appliance or weather or *gesture in the world* even as it's also in the act of helping us make the world new the way small children do."

"The *real* pleasure," said Norval, who must by now have decided that he had given me quite enough time to express my opinions, such as they were, "is to disrupt the rule of the word by breaking open the pure sign of the letter: "k, l, m, n, o...."

The Story of O must have caught Guido Gallo's attention after all, because he was now sitting on the side of my bed with the opened book on his knees.

"...feelings, etcetera," Norval was saying. "But also to *mean* something. For example, I like to write out the narrative of my poems not only with condensed lyric moments, but to string them together in such a way as to *imply* narrative—*saying* that stories themselves, or linearity itself, are a fiction...."

"But doesn't it strike you as significant that the more we stand helplessly by and watch postmodern critics expressing contempt for linearity and stories, the more we're also obliged to watch the lonely writer being destroyed? And the more the writer is made to feel self-conscious about the process of writing and, being self-conscious, the more the writer tries to decipher just exactly what it is that he or she is doing, the greater the loss to art?"

"But the author is dead," Norval said.

"The author is dead, the novel is dead, God is dead, irony is dead, have we left anything or anyone out?"

He smiled a small secret smile.

"One of the most shameful stories of twentieth-century culture," I said in my darkest and most meanly instructive voice, "is the story of how the wrong people—idiots, pretenders, fascists of the academy—grabbed control of the language and smashed it. And besides, couldn't the grandiose tone of your statements be taken to be somewhat self-serving? Since it's a tone implying not only that you have read absolutely everyone, but that you, and only you, are qualified to judge?"

"All I meant is that a brilliant poet is someone who sees language as pure possibility, an attempt to satisfy all our crises with meaning, and that if it's to survive in a world with, for example, great TV, it must unlock feelings that are not yet in the language or common speech to begin with...."

We were now climbing the stairs to the second floor of Concordia's library tower, and when we reached the turnstiles I told Norval that I needed to go into the fiction section to find something to read over the holidays. "And so I'll say goodbye to you now," I told him, "and wish you a happy Christmas. Or, if you will, a happy solstice."

He smiled politely. He could have been a young banker in his sternly tailored dark overcoat.

"Or whatever applies."

"Oh, it's Christmas in my case," he told me. "But I'm afraid that all the festivities and rituals of the season do tend to give me an almost tragic sense of déjà-voodoo."

In the library I found a book that had a photograph of Tolstoy's grave in it. In a swept grey Russian forest, the bier looked like a shy highland sheep dog, long hair hanging down in front of its eyes, it was such a hairy mound of wild grasses, petals and white flowers caught between unkempt strands of grass and scattered across its top. I added this book to the pile of

17

books I was bringing home with me, but as I was on my way down the stairs to the street again, I wondered what Norval had wanted to ask me. I remembered his saying "déjà-voodoo," and the phrase began to seem spookily familiar. I wondered if it was the name of one of the rock bands of the nineteen-sixties, it sounded so playfully bleak. But then Prehistoric Vamoose could be a great name for a band as well.

The elevator stopped on the first floor for Guido Gallo and also for Max, my next-door neighbour on the top floor, who had to make a run for it to squeeze in just as the doors were closing.

Gallo pressed B, and when the elevator, instead of sinking, continued to rise, he turned to me in a fury. "But I need to go *down*!"

I stepped back. Even Max stepped back.

"*Down*," Gallo said again, like a man speaking to his dogs at Dog Obedience class.

"Once it has gone up, the elevator will go down," I said, but then I was immediately afraid that my tone of voice, being offensively soothing, would enrage him. But he only punched the B.

Max, who was doing a residency in psychiatry at the Jewish General, went into a psychoanalytical rant about Gallo on the way down the hall to our apartments. "I was actually afraid he was going to punch you out. I was all prepared to play doctor and bandage you up."

Instead of bringing snow and sleet, the winter kept bringing the city the gift of balmy weather. Weirdly mild days were followed by warm winds, foggy nights. It even rained on Christmas Day. I called my friend Jenny in Toronto to wish her a happy Christmas and also to complain to her about Gallo. "His breath smells of steroids and gin and he comes into my apartment when I'm not here," I told her, "and I can't tell you how frantic this makes me."

"But it's against the law to do that."

"People do things that are against the law every day."

She told me that she'd invited an old boyfriend (who, before she took him on, was an old boyfriend of mine) for Christmas dinner and she was cooking a duck. "What are you doing?"

"Nothing," I said. "Reading. But I called my brother Frederico in Milan last night. In Milano. And I'm going to make a pot of Zuppa Lombarda and lots of bruschetta. I hardly even know anyone here except for some friends of Dino's who were conflicted enough to stay friends with both of us after our divorce. Claudette and Luc. But I think they have other plans."

The story we critiqued on the first class after New Year's Day was by Rebecca. Ordinarily she wrote furious short poems about family fights and gender politics, but on this particular winter afternoon she began to read us a spoof on romantic love. It was called "A Sad Day in the Life of Mr. Elliott," and it was about a Victorian parson whose sweetheart, Miss Cramp, took poison and died.

So she *did* go to Miss Edgar's and Miss Cramp's then, I thought, it's at Miss E's and Miss C's that she must have received her superlative education. Her story, meanwhile, was ending with Mr. Elliott stepping daintily among the graves in a foggy cemetery and searching for a free plot where he might bury Miss Cramp. "But I need a better title," she told us. And so we started calling out suggestions to her. The one I called out was "Across Some Dark Avenue of Plot He Carried Her Body," but Norval went to the front of the classroom and printed his on the blackboard so that we could all see the joke in how "Him" was spelled in "Hymn and Her." And his title turned out to be the one Rebecca preferred. "But thanks for yours, too," she told me. "You can now keep it for your own use."

"Thank you," I said. Although I couldn't imagine the story I would write to accommodate such a title. Norval, meanwhile, was still at the blackboard, holding a stick of chalk in one hand. "One of my aims in this class," he was saying, "is to foreground the more inventive language strategies and constructs, such as the language of the language group." And he proceeded to print 'language' on the blackboard as L=A=N=G=U=A=G=E.

I went to the blackboard to stand beside him. I barely came up to the level of his heart but I made myself smile as I cupped a hand for the chalk. My own heart was thumping terribly, pumped by fear and adrenalin. What if he wouldn't give me the chalk? What if he refused to sit down? And in fact he seemed to be lost in a dream in which he was the one who was teaching the class and I was merely an older student who'd been given permission to audit the course. 'Chalk,' I said, in the dry voice in which a surgeon might turn to a nurse in the Operating Room and say 'Clamp.'

He dropped the chalk into the cup of my hand and returned to his chair, but now I had to think of something to do with it and so I printed in large round letters: TAKE A BREAK FOR 10 MINUTES, THEN COME BACK TO CRITIQUE REBECCA'S POEM ABOUT THE HOLOCAUST.

After everyone came back—everyone except for Norval and two of his sidekicks—Rebecca read her poem aloud, then I asked the class to make comments. When no-one was willing to speak, I called on a bold young woman in an indigo sweater who was sitting directly across from Rebecca. She cast an uneasy glance in my direction, then spoke in a low voice I'd never heard her use before. "Well, it's good," she said. "It's great, really. It deals with an important subject." She looked unhappy. "Tragedy," she said. "Injustice."

When I asked the others if they all felt the same way about it, they all nodded.

I turned to Rebecca. "Your poems are so often very vivid and original," I told her, praising her more than I felt she deserved to be praised, "But this poem seems to me to be stale and predictable. It seems, in fact, to contain every single cliché of the Holocaust: the mountain of spectacles, the lampshades made out of human skin, the soap made out of the tallow and ash of human bodies, all of these outrages we've all read about so many times before."

I could feel the attentive stillness in the room.

But Rebecca's gaze was fierce, evaluating. "It's about my grandparents," she said.

"Yes," I said. "But the problem is that it comes complete with its own certified anguish."

Were the other students even breathing? They, too, seemed to be afraid.

Rebecca, meanwhile, was speaking of one of her mother's brothers (only a baby back then) dying at Bergen-Belsen. "He was only a baby and he was my uncle and he died," she said.

"I'm not for one moment denying the sorrow of that," I told her. "I would be a monster if I did."

Her eyes so clearly told me that I was a monster *now*.

"The problem is this: your poem comes with its own Seal of Approval for legendary suffering," I said. "If this poem had a voice, this voice would say, 'Nobody is allowed to criticize me.' Don't you see this, Rebecca? "

"No," she said. "I don't."

"And writers do quite frequently sit down to write about the Holocaust in a self-important way," I went on, for there was no stopping me now. "They write about it as if to say, 'Now I am a writer and a significant writer, I must be, I am after all writing a poem about a tragic subject.' But the people who were actually there don't write about it this way, the people who just barely managed to survive at the heart of the tragedy don't write about it this way, the people who were there aren't parasites on the host of the Holocaust—'host' being a word out of biology but also, ironically, suggesting a word out of the ecclesiastical lexicon, since it was mainly Christians or so-called Christians, after all, who killed the Jews—the people who are writing like this are romantics about suffering and the unhappy consequence of this is that poems and stories of this sort are so often melodramatic or romanticized or morally shoddy."

As I spoke, I found myself longing to tell her—to tell everyone—that on my father's side of the family I had Jewish aunts and uncles, Jewish cousins. I wanted to cry out, *I too am a Jew!* I wanted to tell her that the uncle known in my family as Cousin Rocco was a member of the resistance against Mussolini in Bologna and that this uncle was caught by the fascists the summer he turned nineteen, then he was taken up into the hills north of the city to be shot. I longed to cry out to my students, "He was a hero, I tell you, a hero! I come from a family of heroes!" But it would be beyond the pale to say such a thing, it would sound horrible, competitive—*my* Jewish uncle was a hero, *your* Jewish uncle was a victim—it would bring the yadda-yadda-yadda of the schoolyard into the classroom, it would be pitting an uncle who was almost an adult against an uncle who was only a baby. And, besides, I didn't have even one drop of

Jewish blood in me, I only had Jewish cousins and Jewish uncles and so I restrained myself.

Rebecca bolted from the seminar-room the instant the class was over, but the others got up from their chairs and gathered their books together slowly. Nine or ten people then left the class in a chattering crowd, just as they always did. But the remaining students filed past where I was sitting. One by one they spoke to me on their way out. "A great class," they said. "Really amazing. The best class all year."

I looked up at them narrowly. "So why didn't you contribute to the discussion, then?"

They stopped in the doorway and looked back at me, then smiled their most sheepish small student smiles.

"Then it could have been even more amazing," I told them. "But you just sat there like a crowd of *mutes*."

Yes, Gina, they said. Sorry, Gina. See you next week, Gina.

Then they were off, down the stairs. "Did she say a crowd of mutes or a crowd of *newts*?" I could hear a male voice ask as other voices were bumping away down the stairway. I could even hear a faraway girl's voice faintly answer, but hard as I strained to hear, I couldn't make out what she said. My heart was still beating too hard and the more I thought about my heated discussion with Rebecca, the more I feared repercussions. We'd already had a number of tense class discussions—God spelled with a big G versus God spelled with a little g being our most passionate fight so far—but I couldn't dwell on it anymore, I had to get organized for a staff meeting at five.

Farley LaRue, the Australian who was the current director of the writing program and also the man who'd hired me, kept watching me while the other instructors were talking. I wondered if he knew that I was more than a little in love with him. I loved his emotional eyes and the self-parody in his voice when he said "Good die" instead of "hi." But he'd probably only been told the story of the uproar in my workshop and so I was left to wonder whose version of the afternoon he had heard: mine or Rebecca's. From the way he couldn't seem to take his eyes off me, I was afraid that it must have been Rebecca's.

He caught up with me on our way out of the staff-room. "I hear that you aren't permitting your students to write about the

Holocaust."

"Not true," I said. "I will only not tolerate bad stories and bad poems about the Holocaust."

"Well, that's good. It's good not to tolerate what's bad. Because God knows we too often do."

"But how did you hear this? And who from?"

"From a very tall white-haired young person. A sort of albino giant."

"Norval Tapp-Hansen," I said. "He's a sociology transfer. But there's a mystery here, Farley, and the mystery is that Norval didn't even stay for the last half of the class today. He left during the break."

"Which would explain why he was able to speak about it with so much authority then." He lightly allowed a hand to rest on the small of my back as we were pushing our way through the swinging doors to the elevator hallway. It was the most fleeting of touches, but as everyone knows, the most fleeting touch is exactly what it takes (and exactly all it takes) to activate days of love thoughts and sexual brooding. "So," he said. "Have there been problems? With this albino guy?"

"Not really," I said. "He's a pretty normal boy, actually. Although it would distress him so much to hear me say so. In his own wacky way, he might even be somewhat gifted. It's just that he's fallen in love with the whirling dervishes out there in the hinterland of critical thought. Or maybe it's not even the hinterland anymore, for all I know it could be the Grand Central Station of critical thought."

It was dark when I came down to the street, and as I was hurrying along Boulevard de Maisonneuve to the metro, three tall men in black coats came walking toward me. As they approached, they moved into single-file and I was startled to see that they were my students: Norval Tapp-Hansen and two of his disciples. In an attempt to deal with the awkwardness of meeting them off-campus, I bowed slightly, then spoke to them as if I were a character in a Victorian novel: "Good evening, gentlemen."

They stared at me, stared through me, then walked right on by while my heart raced at having been snubbed by them. If I had been a male instructor, I told myself, and if I were taller, they wouldn't have dared to ignore me like this.

It was in this frame of mind that I turned onto Grand Boulevard, then took the elevator up to the fourth floor and unlocked the door to my apartment. But as I was letting myself inside, I was shocked to see Guido Gallo standing in my kitchen and talking to someone on the phone (to a plumber, from the sound of it). I stood drawing off my scarf and stuffing my gloves into my pockets as he was saying goodbye to the person on the other end of the line, then he turned to tell me that he'd just fixed an emergency problem with one of the pipes under my sink. "There was a leak in the apartment below." But then he did a really odd thing: he picked up the receiver again and held it out to me.

I looked down at it. It was a white receiver although parts of it were grey and there were also brown blurs on it from where I was in the habit of holding it too tight when I talked on the phone.

"When I look at this telephone," he told me, "I see exactly the kind of woman you are, signorina, the kind of woman who doesn't know how to keep her place clean, who doesn't even know how to keep her *telephone* clean, and it shocks me that you, an Italian woman, do not know these things...."

I refused to accept the phone. "How dare you speak to me in this way?"

"I speak the truth, signorina."

"*What* truth? My apartment is orderly. My telephone is white. I hold onto the receiver, as I must, when I speak into it. To my friends...."

"I know what I know," he said in his smugly ominous voice.

I tried to stay calm, I tried to say in a calm voice, "Do you know what I do?"

"You're a teacher," he told me, squatting to buckle the buckles on his toolbox. "Or so you said on your rental application." And in a horrible assessing way he squinted up at me to study my out-sized black jacket and my white cotton pants with the geometric black fishes swimming downstream into my pointed black boots. "And so what do you teach?"

If I'd told him I was a sessional lecturer he wouldn't have known what I was talking about and so to simplify matters—to simplify matters or to glorify matters—I said, "I'm a professor."

He stared at me, then said in an astounded voice, "You mean like at a university?"

"Yes," I said. "At Stanopolis."

"A very fine school," he told me in a stunned, pompous voice. "My niece went there."

I could all too easily picture her: a brash and cheaply trendy girl with glossy black hair. Thousands of such girls crowded the hallways at Stanopolis every day of the week.

But that night as I was getting ready for bed I had two revelations:

1. Norval and his friends weren't snubbing me, they were avoiding me because they'd skipped the last half of the class. This was why they'd stared blankly ahead when I greeted them, they'd been hoping, in the dim light of a winter twilight, that I would mistake them for strangers.

2. Gallo was not talking to a plumber at all, he was merely shrewd enough, when he heard the sound of my key in the lock, to pick up my phone and solicit plumbing tips from the dial tone.

The next morning I could hear the ticks of freezing rain on the skylight. It must have turned colder during the night. The first thing I planned to do was visit a hardware store to buy the kind of chain for my door that I could lock from the outside with a little brass key. This would keep Gallo out, at least for a time. Either that or I was going to have to find another apartment. I went to a window and looked down on the street. People hurrying along the sidewalks were looking deranged, were wet dogs in their parkas.

I went back to the stove and turned on the element closest to the sink. But there was no pop of blue flame, there was only the tiny and distant roar of the gas. I struck a match to ignite the roar, and the blue flower popped into place. I filled the kettle with water, set it down on the element, then turned on the news. There was no sound. The power was out, then. But how could I even be surprised? Stubby ice had been building up on the twigs and tree branches for days, giving them a deformed

25

look. It was at this point that I also remembered a series of ominous sounds during the night: tree branches cracking, then a series of crashes, followed by tinkling avalanches of ice-casings.

When I called Claudette, on the other side of the mountain, she told me the whole city was out. "Everything except for the golden triangle up on the Plateau. And we, ma chère, are in it. Come and stay with us for the night. Or for however long it takes."

"But is even the downtown out?"

"Everything."

A few minutes past noon I heard a woman's voice in my kitchen. She was saying, "And the really weird thing is that Hydro-Quebec...." But this was as far she was able to get before the power went off again. I opened the top drawer in my desk and counted my candles. There were at least twelve of them, plus a packet of matches. I clicked on my flashlight and it sent out a bright beam of light.

Just past four, I pulled on my raincoat and made my way down the dark stairs, then walked out to Monkland to buy supplies. The Korean store was illuminated by a kerosene lamp and one squat green candle. When I got home again I stood in my front room and looked out over the dark city. There were no traffic lights, no street lights, no lights on in any of the buildings. As far as I could see, there was only darkness. Wartime London must have looked like this.

Although I could get all the gas burners on the top of the stove to ignite, no matter how hard I tried I couldn't light the oven. This was unfortunate, since with a working oven I could have baked bread, cooked up a storm, cooked a goose, baked gingerbread men, all the foods I hadn't bothered cooking for Christmas, and in the process I could have kept my apartment terrifically warm. But all I could do now was boil a chicken drumstick in a pot, then make a salad of cold beans and red peppers and shallots.

When I'd finished eating, I called Claudette again.

"Hydro-Quebec has put its public relations people on the telly," she told me. It amused her to use Anglo words, above all if they were Anglo words that came from England. "They are very severely dressed and make me think of the Spanish Inquisition. You can still come. Come tonight."

But I was sure the power would be on by morning. "My place still has some leftover warmth in it and I'm having lots of hot soup and tea."

After she had finished watching the late night TV news, Jenny called me from Toronto. "Things look so bad where you are. The power pylons are so coated by ice that they are bending over like dancers."

I tried to picture it, but all of my images of power pylons were summer images, from car trips: pylons walking over green hills like Meccano monsters who'd escaped from children's books, each tower a black cat's cradle-design in a child's drawing of a very tall stick figure, the short little arms hanging straight down from all of its (many) straight shoulders, another cat's cradle in each tower's deaconess hat. As I piled my bed with my duvet, three blankets, two winter coats, and a rug, I pictured all these deaconess hats bending to the left, to the right, in obeisance to the northern fields of blowing snow.

The last thing I did before climbing under my mound of blankets was hold a match to the wick of a candle that I'd poked into a pottery vase. Then I set it down in the bathtub. It wavered and smoked, but at least it would provide me with some kind of illumination if I had to get up in the night.

Then I lay in the uneven darkness and thought about a visit to Italy three years ago, to meet my Jewish uncles and cousins. In one of Bologna's main squares, Dino and I stood squinting up until we found the face of Cousin Rocco among all the photos of faces that were displayed like enlarged graduation photographs in the pages of a giant book: a memorial to the members of the local resistance who'd been shot by the fascists.

I also thought of a story I could write about a young Montreal woman who would set out on streets of grey ice for the house of one of her professors to drop off an essay. In her professor's enclave of tall houses, the high snow banks would also be coated with ice. She would throw her coat down on the slippery hill leading up to her professor's verandah but would stumble and fall as she was walking up her coat's silky lining, break an arm, then be unable to worm her way back into her sleeves. And

27

although she would yell out for help, no-one would hear her or see her until two hours later when a car would stop and a man would get out, rush up the icy hill to lift her into his arms, then carry her down the hill to his car, wrap his coat around her because her own coat would be too cold, then drive her fast to Emergency at the Royal Vic. But it would be too late, she would already be near death from hypothermia and when he'd call for news of her the next morning he'd be told she was dead.

I already had a title for it, the title Rebecca had turned down, and because I could already see it as a story in a collection of stories, I could also see it as the book's title: *Across Some Dark Avenue of Plot He Carried Her Body*. But it was also a story that made me want to think of warmer times and so I pictured myself in tropical Toronto. I was running a bath of hot water up to the top of the tub in my former apartment on Galley Avenue. I thought of Norval too and wished that I had cried up at him, "But Norval! Why be a spokesman for the Academy? Why not be on the side of the *writer*? (The writer, dead or alive.) The Academy, after all, is filled with doctrinaire dimwits, with people who want to take all pleasure away from the reader while giving no credit to the writer. Also bear in mind that the best readers *want* the writer to matter, they want to see into the writer's soul, and the reason they want to see into the writer's soul is because it gives them the key to their own souls."

I then began to recite the opening of my novel to myself. Word after word. Like the words of a prayer. MY WORK. I wondered if I would ever finish it. But then I got an idea for a new beginning for it, one that I wanted to be able to remember in the morning:

I am writing this under an assumed name, even though my obscurity—a small thing, but my own—is such that writing under my own name would be quite protection enough. But to get right to the point: I am a teacher. Or to be more exact, I work as a teacher. My other life is lived as a writer. This is where the obscurity comes in.

People would think it a whine, of course, since in the opinion of the whole world, writers are children who do nothing but whine. I could also write about a woman in my situation and make her say to a woman friend, "Out of boredom I've been feeling incredibly oversexed and this has led to at least one fascinating discovery: it's damn hard to make significant contact with your clitoris when you're wearing your mittens."

Then I must have fallen asleep, because at some point an hour or two later my heart began to beat too fast when I heard someone in the next room whistling "Scotland, the Brave." I sat up and opened my frightened eyes to a distant flickering in a contaminated darkness, then remembered the candle I'd set in the tub. By now I also understood that the whistling, although it seemed so spookily close, was actually down on the street. But the contamination seemed to be coming from car exhaust fumes and it was so extreme that my bedroom was smelling like an underground parking garage. I ran over to my window to see if a transport truck was idling on the street below, but I could only feel a fresh breeze that had the smell of thaw in it. I also was able to spot the whistler: a tall man in black slacks and a hooded black parka hopping down Grand Boulevard as he continued to whistle.

The bad air was inside the building then. I hurried to the door that led out to the hallway and opened it a crack, but the air smelled so awful that I quickly shut it again, then shoved an old blanket against it. I carried my candle into the kitchen to look for a roll of duct tape, then went back to the door and taped it with several widths of the tape. The last thing I did before going back to bed was open the door to the balcony so the clean wind could blow in. My favourite tree was still standing. It was as tall as my balcony in the moonlight, its trinkets of ice tinkling.

"People are being urged to go to shelters if they don't have heat or hot water," Claudette told me the next morning. "But you don't need to go to a shelter, you can come here."

"I know. And I really appreciate the offer. It's just that I can't bear to leave my own place."

American soldiers were now being trucked up from Vermont, she also told me, but since there was nothing for them to do they were throwing their financial support behind the sex trade, the stripper strip of St. Catherine Street being one of the few parts of the city that was now favoured with power. "The moral of this story," said Claudette, "is that God loves sin." The downtown universities also now had power, and many of the students and in some cases their professors were bedding down in their sleeping-bags in a number of the offices in the Humanities tower at Stanopolis College, even though classes were still cancelled. I wondered if Norval Tapp-Hansen was among them, he might even be sleeping in the office I ordinarily shared with six other sessional lecturers. I pictured him sitting up in his sleeping-bag and pontificating to the assembled students and professors just before the lights were turned out for the night.

The next morning the walls of my bedroom seemed to be exhaling a deeper and more eternal cold than they had at bedtime. I didn't dress, I was already dressed, but I was so tired that I found it hard to sit up and pull on the kimono I'd inherited from Dino, then tie it on over my raincoat. And then after I'd had my mugs of tea and my bowl of hot porridge, I created pockets of warmth by boiling more water, then I carried it in steaming bowls from room to room, to small shrines of candles.

I was by now wearing (under my kimono and bulky raincoat) a pair of black cotton tights, three pairs of trousers and three sweaters, thick wool socks in my winter boots, and a black woollen hat. I sat down to call a teacher friend from Stanopolis. "Heat up saucepans of water and pour all the hot water into a giant plastic Javex bottle," she told me. "Then use it to keep your feet warm all through the night." I tried it, not for my feet, but for my breasts since my nipples kept feeling cold, and so I ended up sleeping with the hot Javex bottle hugged in my arms like a toxic doll.

Late the following afternoon, toward five, as I was walking into my front room, I saw a sight so astounding that it brought tears to my eyes: the highrise on the far side of rue Terrebonne was completely lit up with lights. The Hydro people were moving my way then. I couldn't believe it. I pictured the way the power would march, block by block, toward my building. Each new light would be another jigsaw piece in a puzzle whose solution would be a hot bath. I said a heartfelt prayer of thanks to God. Never again would I take the comforts of the modern world for granted. I went into my kitchen to make tea, then returned to my big room again. I looked first toward my beautiful tower of lights and saw that it had gone dark. How could this be? Ten minutes later all the lights were on once again, a kind of electrical tease, but by bedtime the whole city was steeped in darkness once more and when I went to look out at my tower at midnight and saw that there were still no lights on in any part of it, I began to feel hopeless, I began to feel that something had gone terribly wrong in some impossible way that could never be mended.

In the morning I had to untape the door so I could go out. Ceiling lights were now on in the hallways, but they were feeble, unstable. Down in the basement, I could hear a tremendously loud motorized racket coming from the boiler-room at the end of the hallway. On my way back up, I met two elderly ladies on the third floor landing. "The generator is letting exhaust fumes back into the building," I told them. But they were ancient, in their nineties at least, and they only smiled at me. One of them was wearing the thick dark glasses of the legally blind, the other one had a hearing aid. I nevertheless told them that I was on my way up to my apartment to call Gallo to complain. "But do you think you might call him too? To tell him that this is simply not acceptable?"

"But darling, how can we," the one who was blind asked me. "When we can't smell a thing?"

And the other one, the one who was so ancient that her voice scratched like the random trajectory of a dry leaf on pavement, said they simply couldn't do it. "We can't, my darling. We need the lights in the hallway so we'll be able to see when we want to go down the stairs...."

When I got Gallo on the phone and he told me that the generator's fan was blowing all the fumes outside the building, I asked him why I could still smell them then.

"There's always some smell from a generator," he told me.

I hurried down the stairs again, then stepped with relief out into the clear air. Ice had fallen from the eaves and, mid-fall, torn through the striped awnings of the stores on Monkland Avenue. The street looked bombed, deserted. Even my Korean grocery store was in darkness. Icicles hung from the eaves. The place looked as if it had been robbed, then burned out.

31

A taxi was making its way down the street. I tried to look human as I hailed it, I tried to look middle class, I hadn't had a shower since Tuesday morning. When the driver stopped, he leaned over and rolled down the window on my side. "Where to?"

"To wherever there's power. I need to buy food."

We drove east toward the metro station at Villa Maria, then across to Vendôme. In the side streets the fallen trees looked like mounds of branches piled high for winter bonfires. Encased in ice or whitened by frost. And every store window was dark.

As I walked along the aisles of the supermarket on Sherbrooke Street, I wondered what my students were eating. I pictured them living on a diet of peanut butter and vodka. My own diet would be more varied: a ham and a chicken, a wheel of Camembert, asparagus, cornmeal for polenta, apples, and five bottles of wine. I pictured Rebecca pouring herself a glass of vodka and despising me, wanting me to come to some harm. I saw Farley too, cooped up with his wife and three noisy children in a tiny house.

On our way west, I decided to ask the cabbie if he would help me carry my bags up to the fourth floor if I gave him a good tip. But what would be a good tip? As we turned onto Grand Boulevard, I made him an offer. "If I give you a five dollar tip, will you help me carry my groceries up to the fourth floor?"

He whimpered with the twisted whimper of a baby wanting to be picked up.

"Six?"

Another whimper.

"Eight?"

A groan that somehow ended up as a hiss.

"Ten?"

A deeply souped-up, self-dramatizing groaning whimper.

"Eleven dollars," I told him as we pulled up to my address. "And that's my final offer."

He lunged out of the cab, grabbed my bags from the back, leaving me to hurry behind him.

I taped up my door again after I'd paid him, then poured myself a glass of wine and drank it down in one swallow. Why hadn't this occurred to me before now? To drink wine? It was a

32

perfect drink for the circumstances I now found myself in, it was the true fire water, it was a sparkling diuretic, it was the burning fuel even doctors now recommended for a healthy heart. I decided I would drink it for the duration, and if the power took too long to come back on again I might even turn into an alcoholic.

I still couldn't get the oven to ignite and so I dumped the ham into a stew pot on top of the stove, then sat near one of the banks of candles, trying to read a book that I'd borrowed from the library in happier days. Someone had written "he" or "she" next to every second line of unattributed dialogue, words that made me think of "Hymn and Her," Norval's title for Rebecca's story about the parson and the unfortunate Miss Cramp.

Then it was morning again, and I could hear a heart-stopping sound: the military clip of boot cleats walking across my hardwood floors. I pulled my blankets over my head and cowered. It would have to be Gallo, only Gallo had a key to my place. Back and forth went the boots. I peeked out from my cave of blankets, then edged out of my bed in my stocking feet and picked up a chair as a weapon. But when I got to my front room it was empty, even though the boots were still walking. It must be Max. I could hear the door of his apartment open, then close again. I ran to my own door. Now the boots were on their way out to the elevator.

"Max?"

There was a puzzled silence, then I could hear Max's voice call out, "Who *is* this?"

"It's Gina."

"Gina! Christ, are *you* still up here? Everyone from up on this floor has moved out."

"I know, but I can't open my door because of the exhaust fumes...."

I could hear his boots walking back to my door. "Exhaust fumes?"

"You can't smell them?"

"No," he said. "I don't think so. But listen, I've got to go now. If you need anything, though, just call me at the hospital, I'll be there until the power comes back, sleeping with the madmen...."

33

Since Max and I lived on different schedules and hardly ever bumped into one another any more, it was a novelty to talk to him like this, through the door. So that once he was gone I felt lonely, especially when I remembered that the Sunday afternoon I moved into my apartment he was the neighbour who came over to help me hang my pictures and unpack my books. He even put a background on my computer screen for me, a bluff of blue trees rising behind a lower bluff of frost-whitened smaller trees, and a few minutes after he'd gone back to his own place I'd turned it on again, and again I'd experienced a sensation of the most extreme sexual relief and excitement, a feeling of lift-off, a sensation of soaring up over the blue forest, the magnificent swoop upwards lifting me above the massed choir of the trees.

"Please call someone," Jenny told me when I talked to her that night. "Please call the emergency number. Although if the firefighters come tonight, they'll probably make you move into a shelter."

I could all too easily picture life in a shelter: women in blue slacks standing at the water fountain of the nearby primary school and squinting against the smoke of their cigarettes as they stood looking the other women over the way the tough girls used to look the other girls over in high school. I also thought of how the air would be heavy with the smell of noodle soup and cigarette smoke and peed-in diapers and vomit. Vomit and fried bacon and cold coffee and cheap jam. I would wait till the morning then. But then I remembered the worry in Jenny's voice and so I decided to make just the one call to the emergency number. When I dialled it, an automated voice told me to call another number. The voice at the next number was also automated, but it gave me the number of the police. I explained the situation to the cop who answered the phone at the police station. "Are you crazy, madame? People are fighting with their concierges to *get* generators."

"But this generator isn't even giving any heat, it's only giving a few weak little lights."

"And you are very disinconvenienced by these odours?"

"I've had a bad headache for nearly four days."

"So what do you wish me to do, madame? Connect you with the fire department?"

"Yes," I said.

The man at the fire department had a tender voice. I knew this because, out of loneliness, I'd become adept at hearing gradations of tenderness in voices. So that when he said, "Where *are* you," putting the emphasis in such an emotional way on the second word, I knew that he practised tenderness in order to extract information from people in trouble so they could quickly be found and saved. But when I gave him my address, there was a pause, he must have been reading it on a display terminal and was understanding that I'd jumbled the numbers, and once we'd got them unjumbled, I said, by way of explanation, "The fumes must be getting to me."

"We'll be right there," he told me.

And soon, very soon, much sooner than I'd dared to hope, I could hear sirens being raced down the dark street below. Oh Lord, I thought, I am in trouble with Gallo now.

I ran to my door and squinted out through the peep-hole at the dim hallway, the flickering lights, then heard heavy boots tramping up to the top floor, saw an industrial flashlight being aimed like a searchlight at my door, heard a stampede of heavy boots running down again. After a few moments, I also heard distant shouting and a series of bangs, then the hallway went black.

I carried a candle to the kitchen counter and set it next to the phone so I could call Jenny. "The firefighters came, and now the lights have gone out, so the generator must have had to be turned off at once, it must have been that lethal."

While we were still talking, I could hear boots and voices coming up the stairs, then there was an imperious knock on my door. "Just a minute," I whispered. "Someone official seems to be here," and I went to the peep-hole and peered out into the dark to see two ghoulish white faces floating above the lights of two flashlights. Two firefighters. But to be on the safe side I lowered my voice almost as low as a man's. "Who is it?"

Gallo's voice called out of the darkness in an accusing singsong, "It's the fire department, signorina! As *you* should know! Since *you* are the one who called them!"

The other voice (the low voice I remembered) had something to say to this, then called to me, "Could I come in?"

"Yes!" I called back. "But I'm afraid it will take a few minutes, I have to untape the door!"

"D'accord. C'est okay."

I ripped the tape away in long strips and when I pulled the door open the firefighter turned to Gallo. "You can go back downstairs again, m'sieur, I don't need you to be here...." So Gallo was banished and I was grateful, even though allowing a representative of the fire department to catch sight of all my piles of books and papers, flanked as they were by sputtering candles, made me feel apprehensive. But the man who stepped into my apartment didn't look to either right or left. "Come with me," he told me. "I want to show you something."

I followed him into the dim kitchen, the candle flames fluttering in the draft he'd brought into my apartment with him. He was holding something that looked like a level, the kind a carpenter might use. "This is to measure carbon monoxide levels," he told me. "But down in the basement of your building the levels were so high that it was not possible to measure them. If your concierge had gone into the boiler-room and stayed for only one minute, he would have died. We had to chop down the door with an axe and go in there with gas masks on. It was a very lucky thing that the generator was faulty enough that you could smell the fumes, since carbon monoxide has no odour. If you had not called us tonight, within 24 hours everyone in this building would be dead." He turned emotionally toward me. "You should be proud of yourself. You saved lives tonight."

I so much wanted to bask in his admiration for at least a minute or two, but I had to make myself say, "But it wasn't me. It was a friend of mine in Toronto. She begged me to call you." And it was only then that I remembered that Jenny was still on the phone. I picked it up in a guilty hurry. "Are you still there, Jen? You heard? You should be proud, you saved lives tonight."

"I heard," she said.

On his way out, the firefighter warned me to be careful during the night. "If anyone knocks on your door in the night, don't open it," he told me. "There is no security downstairs, now that we've had to unlock the doors so the fresh wind can blow in."

After we'd said goodbye, I boiled more water for my Javex bottle and then drank two bedtime glasses of Alezio Rosso. But

I was too excited to sleep. I was too hot, then too cold. I was also getting a sore throat. But I had to keep going back and forth over the events of the evening, I had to keep coming back again and again to Jenny pleading with me to make the call to the emergency number, I had to keep coming back to my decision to not bother to call until morning, then to my final (apparently casual) decision to make the call after all. I hated myself for having been so timid and enduring. If it weren't for Jenny, I could even already be dead by tomorrow morning. And although I tried to examine the syntax of "even already be dead by tomorrow morning," I was by now much too drunk to come to any decision about it. I was also too spooked by a grim hallucination: the view, in the chilled City Morgue, of the long row of dead tenants who'd remained in the building. Fifteen people? Twenty? I was among them, the first one in the row and just as dead and grey and noble as all of the others. But then I thought of another scenario. Because I had taped up my door, I would be the only tenant to live. I had taped up my door, but I hadn't even bothered to call the fire department. I had lived, but the others had died. And because everyone was suing everyone else in the modern world, the families of the dead would pursue me and sue me (it would be a class action suit) and all of my protests, all of my heartfelt cries that I'd called Gallo to complain would do me no good, since Gallo would be useless to me as a witness, being dead. I might even be sent to jail, my life in ruins. I could all too easily see the headline in *The Gazette*: MONTREAL WRITER AND TEACHER SAVES OWN LIFE WHILE OTHERS DIE along with the words that would appear in smaller type directly beneath it: 'This is virtually an act of mass homicide,' a spokesman for the police department remarked at a press conference early this morning....'" I pictured everyone in the whole world reading this story, Norval and Rebecca and Vince and all of my other students and Farley and all my colleagues and Dino and the dean and all of the powerful people in Administration at Stanopolis College. Even the old ladies would not be able to testify that I had warned them, for they too would be dead. But eventually I slept, and in my dreams my throat hurt and I began to cough, then the coughs became shrill as they turned into the sound of the phone ringing and when I

37

reached down to stop these piercing rings, I fumbled because I was wearing my mittens.

It was Gallo. "Because we no longer have the use of the generator, the sump pump has failed, and because the sump pump has failed, the basement got flooded. We need you to get yourself down here and help us bail it out."

I looked across my room at the window. The night was still dark. "What time is it?"

"Six-thirty."

"In the morning?"

He laughed coldly. "Yes, signorina."

"I can't help you, Signor Gallo. I'm too sick."

Claudette called an hour later. The cold winter sun was just rising. "Listen, the forecast for tonight is for way below zero, you could die over there, you could die of hypothermia. And the Inquisition people are saying it could be weeks before power is restored to your part of the city. For God's sake call a cab and come over here now."

I said I would come before dark.

The next time I woke up, the sun was going down and the phone was ringing again.

"Why aren't you here yet?"

"I just need to get something to eat, then I'll come."

"Get here before ten, we want to go to bed early."

"Before ten," I said.

But I hated the thought of the moment when I'd first have to touch the burning cold faucets in the kitchen to run the first glass of burning cold water. I also wanted to think about the firefighter. I pictured a fire in my building and my frantic attempts to gather up all the sheets of my novel. I was crying as I kept forcing them into the refrigerator because the fire was coming closer and all of the other tenants had run down the stairs to safety. But I was going to be saved, my own special firefighter was breaking down my door so he could carry me down the dark stairs in his arms. I was wearing a filmy nightgown and my tan ski boots with the red boot laces unlaced and my arms were hugging his neck, but when we came out into the starry night I could see the pages of my novel, burnt at the edges, flying past us in the dark. A phone was also ringing in a snowbank. I had to make it stop, but I couldn't tell where it was, I was kicking my way through the snow trying to find it, then I remembered that it was on the floor next to my flashlight. I picked up the receiver to stop the ringing, but I was so groggy that it took me a moment to remember what I was supposed to do with it. When I did and said hello, a woman's voice said, "You aren't here yet."

"What time is it?"

"It's eight o'clock in the evening and I'm thinking of calling an ambulance."

"No, please. I'm getting out of bed right away."

I was afraid of the dark out in the hallway, it was such an absolute dark, like the dark in a theatre. I was afraid that when I stepped out into such a deep darkness, someone would be hiding in the alcove to the right of my door and grab me. I practised making my coughs more manly between taking sips of my soup. Then I sprayed lemon cologne all over my clothes and called a cab. I set my flashlight down on the floor and shoved my hands into a pair of high-heeled shoes, then walked the heels in fast and hard little flurries all over the hardwood floors. Then I walked into the front room, stamping my feet in my ski boots and blowing out candles. I wanted whoever was hiding out there to be convinced that there would be two of us coming out of the apartment, or even a whole crowd. My heart was beating too hard when I stepped out the door. I shone my flashlight to my right, into the alcove. There was no-one. I stepped into the smaller hallway at the top of the stairs, feeling dizzy and shining my light down into the bobbing corners of darkness.

Down the stairs in the dark
Night of the Impetuous

O estuary! O regalia!

The moonlight was too bright when I stepped out into the night, and the cabbie, coming down the slope to lift my backpack from me, kicked his heels backwards into the glassy crust of snow to make his descent. When I tried to fit my boots into the small caves he'd kicked behind him, it seemed to me that I was making my way up the hill by fitting my boots into the apertures for the alphabetized letters in a giant edition of the Oxford English Dictionary. And when I ducked into the cab, I could smell how intensely the interior air reeked of a raspberry scent. "How's the driving?" I called, sinking into the sweet luxury of the back seat. "Is it awful?"

"Very bad!"

We swerved down streets that were narrow channels walled by ice, the pavement treacherous, slippy. I called out to him, "What do we do if we meet another car?"

He laughed, then yelled back to me, "We pray!"

Driving along the Boulevard across the top of the city we could see that most of the great old houses were in darkness, only the odd monster mansion had its lights blazing. These were the houses with fireplaces, perhaps many fireplaces. Many fireplaces and a thousand candles. I looked down to see the swarm of hazy lights far below us in the middle of the darkened city, a stirred pudding of tiny lights. I thought of my students down there, their small island of beer and music, their tiny island of warmth, their arguments. No matter what they were actually saying to one another I imagined them thinking *We are a nexus, we are an island of talk in a sea of darkness*, and I wondered if Norval Tapp-Hansen was among them. I could so easily see him down there, could so easily hear him say that the poems I'd brought to class all last fall were pure dreck, that I'd never brought them even one single poem that was worthy of the landfill it would end up in. I also thought of the hot bath I'd soon be submerged in at Luc and Claudette's, and in shaky relief I took a deep breath to inhale the fake raspberry air, then wasn't able to smell it. I lifted my wrists to sniff them and when I couldn't smell the lemon cologne I'd sprayed on them either I understood that the God of Irony had watched over me from the very first night the faulty generator had been turned on, since the timing was so clearly perfect: all the fierce honks I'd made while blowing my nose had made me lose my sense of smell.

Up on the Plateau, I pressed the doorbell for Luc and Claudette's loft, afraid they would see me as some kind of pungent and deranged fugitive from my own apartment, a woman so fattened by sweaters that I hadn't even been able to button up my coat. But they seemed to think I was perfectly normal (or pretended they did) and once we were sitting on low hassocks in their cavernous loft, a space that was vast and utilitarian and hung with immense black canvases smudged by colours like tawny animal skins or streaked by trajectories of dried blood, Luc served us vermouth in smoky glasses so chilled that I had to set mine down on a low table, it was much too cold for me to either drink from or hold, and after we'd sat talking for nearly an hour, I began to experience a desire as strong as sexual desire, and I wondered how much longer I'd be able to make polite conversation when all I could think of was the act itself: taking a bath.

But because Luc and Claudette really did want to get to bed early, the house was soon dark and silent except for one lighted room, the glint of mirrors and shining tiles above the occasional gulp and slosh of water that disturbed the silence whenever I raised or lowered a knee. The room was also wonderfully warm except for the part of it that was near the frosted window next to the tub, a window that exhaled a cool breath on my shoulders each time I leaned forward to add another inch of heat to the bath, then I would slide down to submerge myself in its deep warmth once again while I pictured the window—one of the few bright panes of glass up on the Plateau at this quiet time of night—linking itself to the aggregations of lights in the bars and cafés down in the lower city where my students were, my thoughts of them turning me into a mother lamp attached by an umbilical cord to a distant litter of little lights, and I understood that what I really wanted to do was write a story linking certain episodes with my students to the current catastrophe (the story of how I had not even been the hero of what could have been my own death) and, in the service of this, the big window and the little lights could be the perfect metaphor for the connection.

Luc, who was a technician at Radio Canada, had to leave for work in the early cold dark, but the company Claudette worked for was still shut down and so the next morning we sat drinking coffee at the kitchen table for nearly three hours, sated by sunlight and a marmalade aroma as we passed pages of *Le Devoir* back and forth in an attempt to deconstruct the mysterious bulletins from Hydro-Quebec.

A few days later the story of how desperate the situation had become for the city was written up in all the papers. At one terrifying point—a moment so unprecedented in the modern world that the evacuation of the whole city had been considered—four of the five lines from the north were broken, leaving only one connection linking the freezing citizens to heat and light, a situation that turned Montreal into a lost fortress whose drawbridge made an arc over a moat of snow that stretched over a thousand miles to the castles of power on the shores of James Bay.

When I came back home again five days later and unlocked the door to my apartment, then stepped inside expecting the air to be stale and sour but at least warm again, I was astounded to be met by the rank odour of new paint. All of my pictures had also been lifted down from the walls and stacked on my bed, and on top of the glassed-in photographs and paintings were untidy piles of student work. I walked from room to room, thunderstruck and enraged. This must be unlawful, whatever gave Gallo the idea he had the right to do such a thing? I walked out to the kitchen, looked at the awful green walls, then came back to my bedroom again and gazed in fury at its pink walls, then (to distract myself) picked up the top page to read a student response to an assignment I'd given to the students in both my classes to write a couplet while making use of a slant rhyme:

THE DRUNKARD'S COUPLET

Woke up this morning & took a puke, took a piss,
Took a peek at my ugly mug in my looking-glass

Because this couplet was unsigned, I could all too easily imagine Gallo thinking, She writes garbage like this and she calls herself a professor? And on the next page I found a few incriminating notes of my own, notes I'd made for my novel:

Add the scene where we had sex in the woods in Sweden + two days of bad fights, then reconciliation in sunlit Stockholm, subsequent bladder infection. Do step by step? Or paraphrase? Highlights of Spain can be done via a feverish + hallucinatory memory later on, in Rome or Milan.

42

And so I didn't now only feel invaded, I felt afraid. Fear even upstaged my fury about the new apple-green paint in my kitchen, the polar pink walls of my bedroom. I went back to my kitchen and opened my refrigerator. A salami that the painters (whoever they were) must have eaten with their lunch was rolled up in a thin white towel on the top shelf. A cantaloupe sat next to it. But when I unwrapped the salami, it wasn't a salami after all, it was a paint roller. What idiot had committed this criminal act? But it had to be Gallo—who else?—although at this point I was so weak from hunger that I decided to eat the cantaloupe anyway, because I had to build up enough strength to go down to his apartment and confront him. But after I'd taken only one bite from it I had to spit it out, it tasted so paint-contaminated and vile.

Gallo's wife was the one who answered the door. "Guido tried to contact you," she told me, "but you were never at home. As for the paint odour, it will not harm you, signorina, it has only seeped into the plastic lining of the interior."

That night I walked up to Provigo to buy six boxes of baking soda to use as refrigerator deodorants, but by the next morning there was no improvement and so I knew that I'd have no choice but to go downstairs to tell Gallo I'd be calling the Department of Health if I couldn't be given another refrigerator before nightfall. As I sank down in the elevator to bring him this incendiary message, a little chant kept singing itself inside my head:

Before nightfall
I too am a Jew
Before nightfall
I too am a Jew

I didn't confuse my kind of Jew with either the Israelis or Zionists, I was instead thinking of the more complicated Jews in my own family, my Jewish uncles, my Jewish cousins, along with the Jews of the great migrations of the early twentieth century, the Jews who were the madmen, the neurotics, and the unhappy lovers in the novels written by the Jewish writers I loved. But when I spoke to Gallo, I was so forceful that three

43

hours later he arrived at my door with a nephew who helped him push a round-shouldered old refrigerator they'd found down in the basement into my apartment, then they rolled my contaminated (but much more modern) refrigerator away.

I devised a final test for the students in my bad class that had in so many ways by now metamorphosed into my exciting class. I decided to attach a mark of fifteen per cent to it. It would be an easy mark since I was constructing it in such a way that the answers were revealed within the questions by my having given each question its own introduction:

> 1. On the afternoon that we critiqued Norval's poem, LIFE'S LONG GOODBYE AND THE LAST SPLICED HELLO, I discussed the way the opening words of the poem dropped us right into the middle of the action, and when I did this, I used the phrase 'in *medias res*,' which is a Latin term meaning what?

There were still the students I feared, though, and consequently the Evaluation forms, locked inside my briefcase, kept making the trip back and forth between work and school like contraband. I was waiting for Norval and Rebecca to skip a class. But week after week they attended every workshop.

On the last day of school, I handed out the test sheets and when several people moaned, I told them that a perfect score would add fifteen per cent to the value of the final portfolio. "This test is a gift," I told them, "and so I am expecting perfection."

Danielle, a young woman with bright teeth and bright eyes, then read us long sections from her final story. It was a very good story and, I suspected, mainly autobiographical.

"This story is mainly autobiographical," she told us. "And I've been wondering...there's one person in particular who might recognize himself. My former boyfriend, actually...." She blushed, then laughed a little. "And so do you think he could sue me?"

"Get published first," said Rebecca. "*Then* worry about getting sued."

"Make him into a composite!" someone else called out.

44

"Make him a Greek!"

"Or make him a geek!"

"A writer," I told them, "but I can't remember who, once said it's perfectly fine for writers to write about real people, but that they must take care to have the decency not to publish the person's name and address, above all if they are planning to parody the person or write things about this person that happen to be untrue. What do you think she meant by this?"

"Change the person's looks, change his hair colour, change the kind of clothes he wears. Or she wears."

"Change his gender."

"Give her a speech impediment...."

"Or give him a very small penis," I said.

They all turned to me, stunned, and I could see that they considered me much too old to be making a joke of this sort. "But I didn't actually think of this myself," I quickly reassured them. I even placed a hand on my heart as I said, "It's a joke that's been floating around the literary world for many years by now, the notorious HOW NOT TO GET SUED joke. Of course it only works if the character you're writing about is a man." I looked down at my watch—we only had eight minutes left—and looking up, caught sight of one of my male students writing a quick note, then shoving it over to the (also) male student who was sitting beside him. It would be extremely unwise, I decided, to ask them to share this note with the rest of the class since I was quite certain it was the HOW NOT TO GET SUED joke if you were writing about a woman. And there wasn't really enough time for me to hand out the Evaluation forms, either. I would have done it, I was positive I would have done it, but now there really and truly was not enough time.

Danielle came up to say goodbye after most of the other students had gone. "It was a really great year, Gina," she said, giving me a sideways hug.

Vince, standing behind her, agreed. "This was the class I liked best, this was the only class I really looked forward to." He gazed around the room as if he wanted to remember it. "Very theatrical class," he said in an amused, diagnostic voice. "Some classes are like theatre and you know it's only a gimmick, but this class was like theatre because...."

"Don't stop there," I said. I was feeling that fond and reckless.

"It was theatrical because you...couldn't entirely control it," he said. But then he quickly went on to say, "I know this might sound like an insult, but it's also a compliment."

"I'll take it as a compliment then. And let's just hope my good feelings last until I've handed in your marks."

They laughed, they weren't the least bit afraid of me. Then they were gone and I felt surprisingly bereft. I even found myself wondering if they liked one another, and if their leaving the class together like this could be the beginning of something deeper for them. Danielle's story, after all, had seemed to suggest that she was once again free. Which was when I realized that no-one had asked me about the Evaluation forms. No-one! I had broken the rules and nothing bad was going to happen to me. I stuffed my papers into my briefcase, took one last look at my classroom—*goodbye! hooray!*—then walked out into a deserted hallway that seemed more white and gleaming than ever, now that my students had all hurried down to the street to catch their planes and trains home.

But it wasn't deserted, Rebecca was waiting for me. She was waiting grimly, like the bearer of harsh news. And she wasn't alone. She had a male friend with her, a watchful young man who had acne and suspicious eyes and who'd clearly been told what a total bitch I was.

Rebecca stepped forward and said, "How come you didn't hand out the Evaluation forms?"

I told her that I had carried them to class every Monday for three weeks in a row and that there had never been enough time left over after our critiques for me to hand them out. And that today, ironically, when there *would* have been time, I had forgotten to slip them into my briefcase before leaving home. Under my shirt my skin pulsed, felt damp. What if they decided to overpower me and open my briefcase? But they settled for giving me the sort of coldly satisfied looks that told me they didn't believe a single word I had said.

It was misty when I came down to the street, the kind of day that made me want to talk to myself phonetically, dementedly, "Raspeeghee, Buxtahootha, this is happiness...." But I was really feeling much too uneasy to be happy and when I got home

I called Farley. "Have you got a minute?"

"For you, I do."

"I have a confession to make."

"I'll take your confession."

"I didn't hand out the Evaluation forms."

"Oh Lord."

"What do you think will happen to me?"

"I don't know."

"I'm ideologically opposed to them."

"Tell that to the marines," he said, and we laughed, although my own laugh was shaky.

"I'm not opposed to being evaluated," I told him, "I'm only opposed to the fact that I am being evaluated anonymously."

"Me too." But then he told me not to do anything. "Because while it's true that you might not get your contracts renewed, it's equally possible that no-one in particular is presiding over any of this silliness anyway. Some schools take their student evaluations so seriously that they'll hire and fire on the evidence they find in them, other schools see them as nothing more than a kind of tokenism: give the students this small taste of power, let them vent. But most students are decent people, as both you and I know. Most students aren't vituperative hysterics."

After he'd said this, I remembered that a small group of students had once drawn up a petition against Farley, had collected 25 signatures on it, then rushed it across campus to the dean. The reason: Farley was just too damn demanding and they wanted to ruin him, they wanted a human sacrifice. What saved him was the fact that another group of students got wind of it and quickly drew up a counter-petition and collected an even greater number of signatures, then also swept across campus to visit the dean. Farley told me this whole story himself. He was unable to hold a grudge against the people who'd signed the petition against him, he told me, because to hold a grudge against someone you had to have a good memory and after fifteen years of teaching his memory was shot. But now he was saying, "So let's have a look. I've got the evaluations from the classes you taught at summer school right here."

Flick, flick went the pages as he was turning them.

"I have the feeling that they're fairly polarized," I said. "That

47

I'm either loved or despised."

"You've certainly been despised," he told me. But then he quickly said, "Just kidding, Gina. What I see here, however, is that they seem to be all over the map."

I squeezed my eyes shut and prayed. All over the map was not good.

"But I do also see evidence of real love here."

For a moment I pretended that he was talking about us.

"Not that we should be looking for real love," he said.

"No," I said. And after a small pause I carefully added, "Not from them."

Now the pause was all on his side. But at last he said, "I still say don't let's draw anyone's attention to anything. Let's just wait and see."

O how we know how to speak euphemistically, we who labour in the fields of the Word.

The next morning I rode down in the elevator with a husband and wife who lived on the floor below mine. They were known in the building to be close friends of Guido Gallo and they were sporty dressers: culottes in the palest of pinks for the wife, a visored cap as white as an antacid tablet for the husband. When he made a few comments about the ice storm, then asked me if I'd stuck it out 'for the duration,' I told him no, I'd had to leave because I got sick.

"*We* stuck it out," he said, standing so tall in his pastel uniform that I felt, next to his towering smug blandness, devious and dark and patterned and ironic.

Three weeks later, on a windy afternoon in late May, I was rinsing a bowl of strawberries under running water when I heard a knock on my door. I turned off the gush of water and wiped my hands dry on the hips of my skirt, then called out, "Who is it?"

"It's me, professor! Guido Gallo!"

When I opened the door, he told me that he would be needing my apartment as soon as my lease was up. Or sooner if possible. "For two of my nieces to live in." So this was why he'd painted my kitchen such a sick green and my bedroom such an extreme ice-cream pink, he must have known even then that he'd be telling me to leave.

48

In fact I moved out much sooner than I needed to, since later that same week I found myself an even sunnier apartment in a nondescript yellow brick building that stood next to a park, and one afternoon when I was sitting on a bench in this windy park reading the *Gazette,* I felt the lunge of someone sitting down next to me and looked up to see Max. He'd been up in Nunavut for five weeks, he told me, and when he'd come back south again I was gone. "These two party hounds were out on your balcony. Hounds or houndettes. And you know how some people laugh and the laugh is all you need to hear to know how dumb they are? Just the laughter will do it, you don't need to hear them say one single word, that's the kind of laugh these two bitches were laughing. And you didn't even leave me a note, Gina, you didn't even bother to say goodbye." He rolled up his grey shirt sleeves and squinted at my new building. While he was up north he'd got a deep tan from the perpetual summer sun and his skin seemed to be giving off a distant northern heat. "And so now you've moved down here."

"I did want to write you a note, but I moved out in such a hurry." I peeled a regretful petal of green paint from one of the bench slats. "I also really wanted to go, I wanted to change my fate."

He continued to study me with a watchful seriousness as I was telling him the history behind my eviction. "What a story," he said at the end of it. "A lone woman in Toronto saves the lives of a whole crowd of people in Montreal. What a tale of two cities. And not a tale of two cities that too many Montrealers would want to hear or believe. So the fucker evicted you. You saved his worthless life and all the thanks you get is that the big bozo kicks you out. On the other hand, it makes a weird kind of sense, the guy's got a death wish, I'm convinced of it, he wanted total control, he wanted to go down and he wanted to take all of us down with him, but then you called the fire department and so now he's condemned to live, God help us all...."

I smiled, I was just so happy that I didn't have to live there anymore, I was free.

"But you could sue the bastard. In fact, we all could. A class action suit."

"I don't want to sue him, I want to write about him instead.

In fact I've been thinking of possible names for him, and Signor Tosti is the one I've decided on."

"Nah," he said. "Too much like Signor Testosterone. Or an opera singer. Play it more against type and call him something more dainty and tippy-toed. Something like Signor Fettuccine."

The next afternoon I went downtown and bought myself a pair of grey silk harem pants patterned with rows of what looked like disinterred gold coins. I wanted to live a happier life, I wanted to feel cool silk against my bare skin. I thought I might even sign up for a belly dancing class and learn a few new moves in the choreography of sexual enchantment. But as I was on my way up to the street again I caught sight of Rebecca. She was with one of her girlfriends and they were standing at the entrance to a sari and sarong boutique and were much too involved in wrapping the great scarves of gleaming golden voile and leaf-splashed green silk over their faded shorts and T-shirts to notice me. Rebecca was looking happy in her big black boots and shining sari, though, and not wanting to ruin my afternoon—or her afternoon, either—by stopping to say hello, I hurried on by. Someday years from now, I thought, she'll phone me and ask me to write a reference for her and I'll do it, no hard feelings. In a way I even admired her, I admired people who wouldn't give up, who wouldn't give in. On my way out into the sunlight I also found myself thinking of Norval Tapp-Hansen. Who, oddly enough, had not confronted me about the Evaluation forms. That kind of confrontation would have been beneath him, he would never have tried to see to it that I lost my job. He would rather talk about me behind my back, I thought. He would rather verbally malign me, he would have his own kind of moral grandeur.

The day had turned breezy by the time I came out of the metro at the Villa Maria Convent and so I decided to walk home. But as I was crossing one of the leafy streets going west, I could hear sirens and so I stood at the intersection of Wilson and Terrebonne, waiting for the firetrucks to race by. Back in the days before I'd ever needed help from the fire department, I'd felt, beneath the automatic gratitude everyone feels, a mild sort of contempt for firetrucks: all those urgent horns and sirens. I think I saw them as very large toy trucks and I saw the men who manned them as little boys, as men whose courage wasn't so much courage as it was an infantile bravado. But now that I had a personal reason to be grateful to the fire department and above all to my own special firefighter, I saw that all that bravery was true bravery. I also saw that whether you're a firefighter or a writer, there's a deep but fleeting tenderness you can offer to those who need to be saved or remembered. But only for as long as necessary, then you do need to go on, the feelings need to become impersonal once again. Because by this time you're already on your way to the next fire, the next story.

A Matter of Firsts

Krista Bridge

Your father's New York mistress was the one you met. The exotic one. She used to say, "'Balls' said the queen. 'If I had two, I'd be king.'" That was her expression, whether something irritated her, like losing her keys, or whether there was a pleasant surprise, like one last piece of birthday cake in the refrigerator. Balls, said the queen. Your father tried to correct her usage. The phrase had exasperation in it, he claimed, and was appropriate only as a response to something negative. She said, "Perhaps you're right," and smiled, but you could tell she was not the type to capitulate in action.

Of course, it was not open to you that she was your father's mistress, although you clearly knew, and they knew it. Your father often went to medical conferences in New York, and he couldn't tolerate hotels, their bed sheets gave him a rash, so he stayed with her—Ella, an old friend from medical school. This is what he told you and your mother, although there was an impish smirk about him when he said so, a conspiratorial wink, as if such patent untruths, and the acceptance of them, were in keeping with the true spirit of family. Three times when you were thirteen he took you with him to New York because your mother had to look after your grandfather, who was in and out of the hospital. Around you, they acted stiff and professional, no sly looks or illicit touches. Of course, the minute you saw her, you knew she was no doctor. It was the body that halted your gaze. Unexpected: its creamy fatness, so graceful, so much itself, that it challenged thinness everywhere. A fatness impossible to reduce with euphemisms. A soothing romantic welcome. This body rolled out of itself. Said, I am the way to be.

52

She lived in the Bronx, on a quiet dead-end street lined with trees, in an old brick house with high ceilings and a rickety wood porch in the back. The air smelled like freshly cut grass and homemade shepherd's pie. On the other streets in her neighbourhood, the air smelled like fried food and smoke, traces of cumin and paprika drifting by on the breeze. You could hardly see to the sky. Everywhere you looked were apartment buildings with fire escapes zigzagging down the crumbling brick. There were groups of teenagers lounging on front stoops, yelling at each other in languages you didn't understand. Your father wouldn't even let you walk off Ella's street alone. Her house was big enough for a family of eight, but she lived there by herself. She had bought it with her first husband, who had left at her request two years later, gladly signing the house over to her because he hated the way it felt empty no matter how much furniture they bought, the way their voices echoed in the large square rooms. He said that people start off with a backyard vegetable garden, not an acreage of farm: a marriage needed a small, fertile space in which to grow. Ella said to you, "There is no such thing as being prepared for marriage. I was prepared. But not that prepared."

She told you that she dated her husband for seven months, and then one night during a walk through the park, he got down on one knee and proposed (This was an essential part of the story, the getting down on one knee. It exposed their romantic folly, the traditional gestures that failed to pan out into traditional emotions). He had no ring at the time, and insisted that a store-bought engagement ring wouldn't be good enough for her. He would fashion his own with the minimal help of a jeweller. For the next two months, he drew up sketches hour after hour in his tiny apartment. He picked up pencils in restaurants and brainstormed plans on greasy napkins. Six months later, the ring still was not made or even in the works. The sketches had been abandoned and he said to her one day, "You don't really want an engagement ring, do you? It's such an extravagant expense." And she had said no, of course not, she was not an envier of diamonds.

They got married not long after, with plain gold wedding bands, and went on a honeymoon to Key West. It was on that honeymoon that she was reluctantly, forcibly, made aware of what the engagement ring incident just dimly foreshadowed. She and her husband went out to dinner one night to a restaurant that was dusty and poorly lit. It was on a narrow downtown street, a street with no other shops or restaurants on it, and there were flies on all the tables. Her husband was always on the look-out for the cheapest restaurant, always had an eye out for a deal. They ate the same dinner, the same food, crabs and black-eyed peas, but he was violently sick later and she was fine. They were sitting in the hotel-room, and he was shivering, crouching on the bed with a blanket wrapped around his shoulders. Then he took off for the bathroom.

He was there for a long time and she was on the bed reading a book; she was absorbed and couldn't divert any attention from *Sister Carrie*. After a while, she thought maybe she should check on him to see if he was okay. What she saw, across the long, narrow bathroom, was her new husband naked, on all fours, vomiting into the toilet. He had all his clothes in a neat pile at the door, and he was naked and heaving. On all fours. She had the back view. She told you it shook the foundation of her belief in what she was doing, this perspective like an aerial view of his penis hanging down, his scrotum tightening each time he heaved. An aerial view. In every word he spoke after that, every touch of his hand, she saw the aerial view and, with it, the chipped affection, the shock of revulsion, the bitterness and fatigue—the detritus of a 30-year marriage—piling at the door of their week-old union. She even made an unsuccessful attempt to book a plane ticket home. She saw the direction they were headed in, the headiness, the glorification, the dependence, then the genital views, the aborted optimism. The triumph of the unflattering. Only 22 and married for three days, she already knew that one corner of her marriage was over, the corner in which she stored hopes of rescue and release, where she still believed ecstasy could be a daily event. Before she left, her mother told her, "There are things that scare women on their honeymoons. No matter how long you've known him. There are things that will scare you and make you want to come home. You can't come home." She was prepared. But not that prepared.

This story, combined with her favourite expression, caused

you to see her as a woman eminently concerned with balls. In those days, vulgarity and glamour were inextricable in your mind, bound together in all things attractive. There was nothing in these early exchanges about genitalia that troubled you. Already you had separated your relationship with her from her relationship with your father. The story about her honeymoon helped you understand why she liked your father, why being with a man as remote as him was freeing to her when it was only oppressive to you. But everything else about them was separate. To you, she said, "Love is a euphemism for lying. Falling in love is lying to yourself. You think you're falling in love with someone, but really you're falling in love with someone wanting you. Bear this in mind." And you did, for years and years.

The other thing you bore in mind for years and years was the first time you saw her, standing on the front lawn of her house under the shade of a willow tree, looking exactly the opposite of what you had imagined. As you sat next to your father on the plane to New York, you pictured a woman who always wore red pumps and silk dresses. You hoped for a cool elegance, a high-heeled woman rarely affected by heat. Shiny straight hair. A doctor's air of presumption, that New York woman's mix of candour and detachment, deserving. It was July, and in fact the mistress was sweating so profusely that she looked as if she had just stepped out of the shower. When she looked at you, you could not help but smile. Married men do not introduce their children to their mistresses. You knew this. There is a wrongness about it—a cheeky, bald-faced wrongness—but somehow the mistress' fatness made it right.

"The gap between your front teeth is about the width of a cracker," the mistress said. Just like that, even before her name. She extended her hand palm down, as if waiting for a kiss.

The name "Ella" made you think of a beachy calm, sustenance and refreshment.

You could not stop smiling.

Leaning against the willow, she stared at you with mellow concentration, as if she were holding a ruler up to that gap, approving of these places you broke off more than the places you stayed together. A look that transformed your plainness into something less neutral. You tried to imagine how she might be seeing you, but you could not settle on something reliable. Whenever you heard a recording of your own voice, you thought it sounded juicy and plump, like the voice of an ugly person. When you saw yourself in the mirror, you looked much wider and lumpier than you realized. This always disturbed you, not because you were less attractive than you hoped, but because of the constant misleading of self, the inaccurate cataloguing of your own value, the predictable return to foolishness. While Ella looked at you, you tried to stand erect and forthcoming, like someone open-hearted, yet discriminating. You worried she might just see a sogginess, a frizzing that wouldn't be tamed.

"Lovely," she said. "Just lovely."

On that perfect hot day in the honeyed laziness of air that doesn't move, at the age of thirteen, you learned what it might feel like to be memorized.

On one of the New York visits, you heard them in Ella's bedroom at two o'clock in the morning. It was the only time you ever heard them together. They didn't say much, but each sound was lined with erotic urgency, a moody pulse. The tender coercions of love. The mistress was a woman who knew how to say baby. Like she had thought things over, and it was the only word she could come up with.

You always thought of her as the exotic one. But why? It was more than the New York accent, which made you think of chipped teeth and long, black hair. It was more than the way she looked, the skin stretched to excess and the mop of sandy curls. She rode her bicycle, with its wicker basket on the front, everywhere she went, and despite her weight looked as nimble as a child, almost as if her weight helped her achieve balance, that Southern lady's sense of unhurried pace. These things you admired. They made her watchable. But the exoticism came from somewhere else. It seemed to you that she'd had so many lives before the one you knew her in.

On your first morning in New York, as you ate breakfast, she told you about the honeymoon with her first husband, about the aerial view.

"Men can do such things to you," she said. "You have to be so careful, careful not to let yourself go too much. Sex especially, honey, watch out. You're so young; your emotions will get involved. It's a matter of firsts. That's all."

She told you about how, as a child, she would lie behind the living-room couch all day. The sun shone down just so through the front window, and she lay there. Her sisters would fight over dolls and sweaters while demanding sandwiches and forming accusations, and her mother would come up with activities to keep the fighting to a minimum, arts and crafts activities like painting their own stained glass. Ella stayed away. She was that contented behind the couch. Only when communication was absolutely necessary did she send out word. She delivered notes through the dog. *I vote hamburgers for dinner. Would someone be so kind as to send a glass of water? It is not true that I got my math test back last week and failed.*

"I called him my own personal Purolator courier," she said. "He would take the notes in his mouth and drop them at my mother's feet."

Her second husband had been a photographer for *National Geographic* and he had been to Africa, he had flown his own small plane over Kenya. You thought that she probably had no use, ultimately, for your father and you greatly respected her for this.

You asked what it was like, living in the house where she had planned a future with her first husband.

"The first week after he left, my furnace went out and I could not get a man in to fix it for a week. It was so cold that frost flowers were forming on the windows, and none of my blankets did the trick. I discovered when I was cleaning that my husband had forgotten just one belonging, his red sleeping-bag in the back of the closet. So for all that week I had no heat, I wrapped it around my shoulders day and night. And I moaned and wondered if I'd made a mistake and I cozied up under that sleeping-bag as if it were the man himself. After the furnace man came, I cranked up the heat and sweated it all out. I put the sleeping-bag back where I found it and haven't looked at it since."

She filled the copper kettle with water, passed her hand under the tap, sprinkled water on the burner and relaxed against the counter as it hissed, as if that was the only end her story needed. "I'd rather be trampled by a horse than ground up slowly by nostalgia."

57

In the sunny kitchen, she was naked under a lace nightgown and you could see everything. You hadn't seen your own mother naked since you were four or five, but it took you no time to adjust to Ella's failure to cover up. There was your father's mistress in the kitchen cooking, and there was her entire body. Your father had once said about her, after an argument, "She's in fine form." And this hadn't made you think of debates at all, of feisty opinions and an unwillingness to back down. It seemed to refer to her body. Such fine form. She walked around, smiling at you from time to time as if she had no idea her nightgown could be seen right through. The rolls of fat, like bread dough. You wanted to squish your hands in and feel the warmth. Your father had already gone off to his conference and he was gone all day. She made you an omelette, with Brie, portobello mushrooms, tomatoes, and spinach.

"We need to fatten you up," she said.

You felt she was taking responsibility for you, tending to you. Normally, you picked at your food, and your father talked about how all the women in his family had no fat on them, they were as thin as could be. He said this with a bit of mocking, as if you were all silly for being thin, but it was clear that he was proud too, proud to be affiliated with this clan of rigorous, thin women. But you stuffed your omelette in quickly and asked for more. You wanted her to see that you were not like most people: you approved of fat, curbs of skin folding, one onto the next.

Ella's face was round and lineless. Your mother was bony and gaunt. You did not want to be associated with her murky demands. She held her past tightly, refused to distribute childhood stories as entertainment. Although you made these comparisons, sitting in Ella's kitchen as she talked in her lace nightgown, they did not mean you saw Ella as a more desirable mother. That was not how you saw her.

A man knocked on the front door, and she reached into a closet in the kitchen and pulled out a bathrobe, wrapped it tightly around her before answering. So she must have been aware then, she must have been aware of all that could be seen.

You were just a child. How can it grip you even now, after all the men, the men and the years?

Later that first day, she took you over to a local outdoor swimming pool. She wore a wide-brimmed straw hat and didn't swim, but sat on a lawn chair waving to you when you looked her way. She was wearing another lace top, but this time she had a shirt on underneath. The pool was full of people, so you couldn't swim properly, but you tried your best to look as if you were cavorting around, having a good time. The sun was hot, beating down on the water so that it felt like a bath. There were no trees around, just a parking-lot on one side of the pool, an apartment building on the other. You snuck looks at Ella and hoped she wouldn't notice. You took water into your mouth and streamed it out through the gap in your teeth.

You wanted to call out, "Come swim with me," but you hadn't the courage. She looked so serene in her straw hat.

When you were ready to get out, she wrapped a fluffy pink towel around your shoulders, then followed you into the change-room, which was a large cement area with no private, curtained areas. You tried to change from your bathing-suit into your clothes without showing your body and without looking as if you were hiding it from her. By accident, you dropped the towel when you went to put on your bra. It was your first bra, and you were not an expert at getting it on and off. So surprised were you to find yourself standing before her, watching calmly, that you simply stood there topless, exposing breasts you were barely familiar with yourself.

Ella said nothing at first. It occurred to you that all you would ever want from love was someone to call you baby, to say it at the lowest pitch of longing and regret.

Finally, looking at your stomach, she said, "You have a scar."

The year before, you had had your appendix out. The scar seemed new, still pinkish-purple. She leaned in and traced an index finger over the thin raised dash, still tender in the way that scars with a history never quite stop feeling tender. You hadn't let your stomach be seen since the nurse held your hand in the recovery-room as you cried with anaesthetic nausea and unanticipated soreness, the awareness that something had been removed that could never be replaced.

But you stood there with Ella as her finger skimmed over your scar. You closed your eyes and held your wet bathing-suit against your leg so that the water trickled down your thigh.

The fingers have a memory far longer than the mind's.

After dinner, your father wanted you to give a recital of your Grade 8 Royal Conservatory pieces. In her living-room, Ella had an old Steinway grand piano, barely in tune, with heavy ivory keys. Your father always organized concerts of this kind, after elaborate family dinners on Christmas and Easter, mobilizing aunts and uncles and cousins and grandparents into the living-room for an impromptu piano recital. For days before, he would hound you into extra practice, then on event day would find himself at the dinner table folding his cranberry sauce stained napkin, the thought occurring to him just then that they might all enjoy a musical interlude. You would play your pieces from List A through to List D, then the two studies, waiting after each for your family to clap obediently like a symphony audience, waiting, after the second study's final note, overdramatized with a pedal sustained too long, for the lone "Bravo" to issue from your father, standing in the doorway.

The same you did for Ella. Only she didn't clap and even your father seemed embarrassed by his "Bravo" in an audience of two, as you kept your foot on the pedal and the sound of the final, off tune A flat of Study No. 3 hummed in the air.

"I'll teach you a real piece," she said. "Something worth knowing."

She nudged you off the piano bench and pulled from inside it the yellowing pages of Debussy's *La fille aux cheveux de lin* and set them before you.

"But it's Grade 9," you objected.

"It's slow. You can learn it."

The following morning, after your father left, she went through it with you, telling you where to pedal and where to create the *legato* with just your fingers. She corrected you at the end, when you played the reprisal of the primary melody too loudly.

"Softly," she said. "As if contemplating."

You played it every hour on the hour twice, and when you performed it for your father on the last day of the visit, you let the music fall from the stand because your fingers held the tune.

On the second visit, you got the flu. You lay in bed sweating and shivering, and Ella took your temperature and murmured in concern. She blotted your forehead with a soft flannel blanket. Your temperature went up to 102, and Ella called your father at the conference hotel and got him out of one of his seminars. Over the phone, he suggested a cool bath. She came into the guest-room and put a hand on your cheek. You opened your eyes but could barely see her because the window was at her back. There was just her silhouette, the sheer white curtains rippling around her.

"You need a cool bath," she said.

You stood and allowed yourself to be led to the bathroom. So weak you felt, so glad to be weak. She held your hand as if she was initiating you into something.

The bathtub was a large, claw-footed tub and the water in it looked clear except for specks of rust, barely visible. Dust floated in the stream of sun through the window. She undressed you then. You leaned against her as she pulled your nightgown over your head, as you stepped out of your underwear. You rested against her arm as she helped lower you into the tub.

You were sweating, and she turned on a fan and set it in the doorway.

"You'll have hot and cold on your skin now," she says. "You'll like it. I know your skin."

Ella kneeled and leaned against the white porcelain, wet her hands. She held you forward gently, your chest against her forearm, while she spooned cool water up over your back. Then she reached for the soap and held it gently while it glided over your back, as if it were soaping you itself. Lifting your foot, she rubbed her thumb along its bottom, and she worked the soap between her hands and made hills of lather along your arm. She hummed.

"I could wash your parts all day," she said.

She did everything for you. Soaping you with conjugal diligence, she held a wet washcloth against your forehead and made sure each part got as clean as the others. She cupped your foot as if she was measuring its exact weight. Then she rinsed you, making waves in the tub and letting the water lap against your breasts before she scooped it into a small wooden bowl and poured it over your head, shielding your eyes with her hand.

61

"There you go, baby," Ella said. "Clean as clean."

That evening you spent on the couch covered in an old afghan, afraid to be alone in your room because every time you closed your eyes, you could see, through the dark inside of your eyelids, enormous black birds with long, trailing wings gliding over your head. Ella made you chicken noodle soup from scratch, and you hoped that your father wouldn't arrive and make a fuss that you were spreading germs in the communal areas of the house. On the coffee table was an old photograph of a balding man with a younger, black-haired woman looking formal and legitimate in a wedding photograph beneath an overgrown oak tree.

"Who are they?" you asked Ella when she brought you a bowl of soup.

"My parents."

"They have a grumpy look about them," you said. "Like someone's forcing them to apologize."

"I suppose they do, don't they?" she said, looking at the picture curiously, as if she had just spotted in a crowd the person she was searching for.

Her mother was Canadian and had grown up in Windsor, she told you, and her father was an American living in Detroit, and they met when he was visiting relatives in Windsor for the summer. For their first date, they arranged to go see a matinee of *Guys and Dolls* across the river in Detroit. She had suggested meeting him at the drugstore on the corner of his street. She was liberated before women were liberated, Ella said. Also, she knew that making an impressive entrance meant more than just sweeping down the stairs while your date stood at the front door under the eyes of your father. She was a woman who knew her entrance. She did not go to the trouble of hot rollers and her bangs taped to her forehead all night for the sake of one mere boy. She dressed for her larger public. An entrance meant a bevy of turned heads; it meant all eyes, male and female, compelled to take her in; it meant the odd reverential whisper passed between strangers. And so she swung open the door of the drugstore and stepped inside and, agreeably, it was as busy as she had hoped it would be. She stood expectantly at the door, wearing a trench coat buttoned to her neck, the collar up around her throat, and the belt pulled as tightly as the need to breathe would allow. She registered Ella's father registering the turned heads, the hushed comments, and was satisfied.

He announced that he had to drop a book at his aunt's on the way out of town and off they went. Up in the old aunt's apartment, the heat was stifling, and the aunt repeatedly invited Ella's mother to remove her coat, and Ella's mother repeatedly refused. The aunt had set out cookies and tea, so they were obliged to stay for a time and be entertained. For half an hour, the aunt encouraged Ella's mother to take off her coat and for half an hour she declined, until sweat was forming on her upper lip and beginning to drip down from her carefully set hairstyle. Finally they left, and in the car, Ella's mother took off her coat, right there on their first date, revealing that she had on only her bra and underpants. Then she rolled down the window and fanned her forehead, checked her hair for signs of humidity in the rearview mirror.

"You see, back then, all the latest fashions were in the department stores in Detroit. You couldn't get them in Windsor. My mother thought she didn't have anything grand enough to wear to the theatre in Detroit," Ella said. "So she planned to go into the department store before lunch, buy a fancy new dress, and wear that."

Your father had come home from the conference halfway through her story, and stood in the doorway still holding his briefcase.

"It was a nicer time then, don't you think?" she asked. "You could take your coat off and let a boy see your bra and underwear and it wouldn't proceed to God knows what else. He wouldn't assume. That was probably the happiest time they ever had."

Your father set down his briefcase. "I thought we were against nostalgia."

"It's not nostalgia. It's just remembering," she said.

They went into the kitchen and left you staring at the Steinway grand.

Is it nostalgia or just remembering when you still play, twenty years later, "*La fille aux cheveux de lin*" without missing a note?

You never did feel that love enriched your life. Mostly all it did was remove the finer points of happiness.

Walking alone on a tree-lined, windy lane in the country. Floating on waves in Miller Lake, looking up at the cliff face. Lying in bed at night, preparing to sleep, preparing to stay awake.

There are experiences diminished by companionship.

It was your father who said this first, but it was a long time before you realized how true it was. He was going to the botanical gardens, and Ella wanted to go along. She hadn't been in years. He said she had to stay with you, you were too young to be left alone in a strange place. "She'll be fine," Ella said. "She's not a child." She looked at you gently, but regretfully, as if you alone were keeping her from something she very much wanted. They stepped into the next room, but you could still hear them.

"I prefer to see it alone." His voice made it clear that he had long since decided. You wondered if he had already moved on to the next one. Even then you understood that there is always someone ready to step into your place.

"We could experience it together," she offered.

"There are experiences diminished by companionship."

She came back into the room, looked at you, and delivered her expression, but sadly this time, without its usual bite.

"'Balls,' said the queen. 'If I had two, I'd be king.'" She rolled her eyes jokingly, but couldn't hide the sadness in them, in the downturn of her lips.

And even though she must have resented you, even just a bit, she was good to you when he left. She made iced tea and filled the glasses too full, so that when she dropped in ice cubes the liquid overflowed. She laughed as she mopped up the counters. You didn't blame her for wanting to go with him. Already, you understood how it must be to feel you'd give almost anything for half an hour alone with someone.

She took you to a park near her house. There was a small group of older Asian men and women practising tai chi on the grass. At the far end, there was an area of thick trees, and she led you toward it.

"This part used to be all trees. Then they cut them down. Here, it used to feel like a forest in the middle of the city. They were so thick, you could stand in the middle and it would be dark. The sun didn't come through. There are trees in there great for climbing. I'll wait out here on the bench. Go have fun."

Through the darkness of the heavy shade, you could see a tree with solid branches low to the ground, moving up the trunk as close together as steps. This tree you climbed and sat on a branch with a U-shaped curve like a seat. The ground was carpeted in rust-coloured pine needles and the air was dark and cool. You leaned against the trunk and looked out at Ella sitting on the bench, gazing across the park at something you couldn't see. That morning, you had sat on the toilet while she had a bath. She soaked for half an hour, running more hot water when the water cooled. When she was ready to get out, she pulled the plug and stayed in the tub, humming, while the water got lower and lower. From where you were sitting, it looked like she was rising up to the surface of the water, floating there.

She gave you presents when you left New York. A collection of poems by E.E. Cummings, a Bessie Smith CD tied with a purple ribbon, a plastic heart pendant, a stuffed walrus. Your favourite: a tarnished silver comb, embedded with tiny coral and amber stones, a family heirloom.

When you married your husband, you wore it in your hair. Something borrowed.

The Organic Milk Rapist
Darryl Whetter

Although more voluminous, the ball-gag, ratchet straps, dam and lube went into the black knapsack's smaller front pocket so Kyra's eggs could go in the rear. The carton was snug (Ferdinand's Free Range!!) and could have borne the minor weight, but who knew, the blindfold could land on him tonight. Martin understood that separate was best.

From the deeper shadows behind a dumpster he waited for the sidewalk to clear and stared up the fire escape to her corner of the building. As promised, the service door was propped open, and its tall crack of fugitive light kept him hard as he crossed the lot to climb the gridded metal stairs, fucksack loose on one shoulder.

Because he was an ad manager and she an unpaid intern, they worked in a landscape of raised eyebrows. Whatever this was that was happening—naked this, hunger this—could only have happened here in the same neighbourhood, at night but not all night. No incriminating sunlight, no recognizable car out front, his face down-turned into an old jacket as he walked. It was spring, and sunlight dogged these polite vampires later each day in this red-brick neighbourhood of tugged curtains and ringing phones. Sequestered by day, they were all business as soon as he arrived each night.

Sweat finally cooling, language and street noises returning, he watched her head rise slightly with his ribs as he spoke. "So Cindy Crawford's on a plane that crashes. She and Ordinary Dude Mike wash up on a deserted island, only survivors. Days turn to weeks. They replace their canopy of leaves with a proper hut, start catching the fish. Amazing what supplies wash up. And, well maybe they don't fall in love, but they sure pass time the old-fashioned way. The weeks grow and she notices Mike becoming unhappy, this despite food, shelter and good sex. When she finally asks him about it, he interrupts her and asks if she'd wear his shirt, his pants. Okay Mike, if this is really— Wham, he's out of the hut, returns with a baseball cap. Tuck your hair up into this. Holding her by the chin he writes *Steve* across the brow of the cap with a piece of charcoal. 'Okay,' he begs her, 'walk down the path. Just keep walking.' She does, but she's a little worried."

"In a ball cap, who wouldn't be?"

"Alone, nervous, she walks and walks. Suddenly Mike leaps out of the bushes, grabs her by the shoulders and yells, 'Steve, I'm fucking Cindy Crawford. I'm fucking Cindy Crawford.'"

"Har har."

"Well Steve, this is great, I mean fucking phenomenal. But we have to keep up the poker faces."

"Poker face. Poker front. You keep up that micro-management and you can poke her anywhere you want." That grinning kiss.

A flash of character, not thigh, had ruined him at the office. When she began stepping past protocol and the vocab *du jour* he saw a gem-cutter's mind. "Who is our customer here?" she asked a think team, and the scythe of her jaw began mowing him daily. When, walking away from a meeting, she turned to him and said, "What's with all the clapping here in Dogville? Pass me the puck and let's go," he was trapped, further imprisoned in her infinite legs. Two days later he overheard her say to a fellow intern, "I thought we were dealing with actual problems, not invented ones." As soon as she was alone he stepped out of his office to invite her to drinks on Saturday night. Immediately he regretted the invitation, not yet because of any fear of her joining him at two pub tables crowded with colleagues, but because of the literal, not the legal, company, the conversations he knew would be about television, not novels, about actors not acting.

Watching her enter the pub and see them then him he felt a soft hood fold up, a tunnel spring the room. Was it his arcing tunnel or theirs? Minutes later when he feigned discomfort in his seat, broadcasting isolation in the arrangement of chairs, she moved back to include him. His single, disastrous mistake was switching to water. If he had continued along the path to paralytic intoxication with the others and then left with Kyra, no-one would have cared. No, he left early and sobering, casually holding open the door for her, and that would never wash.

He had smiled when he stepped around the rear of the cab. And yes, there was presumption in that twinkling grin, but, he hoped, he prayed, it was mutual presumption. The fast kite needed two strings.

Now, waiting until dark, knitting himself into the shadows, chin and brow lowered to his black clothing, he kept his eyes roaming, cleaving distant body shapes into colleague and non-colleague, dreading every Volkswagen. The paranoid quadrant of his brain, the income-deducting, Krantz-shirt-returning, no-more-Josef-Siebel-footwear side of his brain assumed anyone he saw in her building could wind up on the witness stand six months later. (What crime, though? Being in her building?) Some nights, silently climbing the fire escape, he had looked down past his curling shoes to people passing obliviously on the sidewalk below. At the top, heading for that vertical strip of light, he had learned to edge closer to her kitchen window to avoid the shriek of metal waiting in a loose section of catwalk. Streetlight from the window beyond her dark kitchen revealed a squat teapot randomly dialled on the counter or a crumbed cutting board, a stack of dirty dishes or a row of clean. Fingerprints then fingers whole.

If they'd been permitted a Sunday stroll or a movie or a restaurant meal, they might not have reached for the bottom drawer fantasies so quickly. Hunkered into her apartment of vintage trunks and hex-key furniture they were always pressed together on the couch, they were voices in half-lit rooms. She was already out of a bra and into pyjamas.

With so many hours of empty, horny sunlight, they were sending each other six or seven f-mails a day.

From: kyra.houston@clickthink.com
To: martin.tull@clickthink.com
Subject: 'tzo doc

Karen asked me to send you these Metzo
proofs.
Enjoying the weather? It was still hot out
yesterday when I stopped to collect my mail.

From: kyrmeleon@hotmail.com
To: escapethefire@hotmail.com
Subject: my working week and my sunday rest
What did Auden say, dismantle the sun? All
penny pinching winter I've wanted to prop
the sun up as long as possible and now I want
to dunk that silly ball. Let my plants die.
Let me grow pale in grey rooms to speed your
bite and pull.
How do I get this pussy through a day?

By silent, mutual consent they quickly began scripting each
night before he arrived, trading drafts, smuttily asking for clarity, punning endlessly from In-boxes to doors ajar.

I'll be reading on the couch, heels up, door
unlocked. Don't knock. Don't speak. Just
drop.

When, eyes closed, she finally let the neglected book drop and
straddle her tingling breasts, she gloved a hand in his dark hair
and he chuckled at the spine *Middlesex* stiff in her cleavage.

The next night, her hair in one fist, his other hand whacking
ass to the finish, he collapsed onto her slick, heaving back as
uncertain of whose idea was *fist*, whose *smack* as he sometimes
was as to which mouth was his, who tailored the lick under the
arm, who wore it.

"Jesus, how rough do you want it?"

"Well, rape me."

Martin couldn't say he got the first alarming call from Davis at
the precise moment he was thinking of Kyra, of gravity and
reach, of laugh and legs, because he was literally thinking of her
all the time. In the religion of her, in this totality of want, there

69

were no mere moments. Lust-dumb, he was content to push elevator buttons, listen to colleagues, write his lying copy. When Deborah called Martin to say Davis would stop by *his* office, panic did momentarily bleach Kyra from his mind, but of course the sudden fear of being punished for fucking Kyra quickly re-introduced the thought of fucking Kyra. He was half-hard when Davis knocked on the door-frame.

"Martini, how about a chat?"

"Sure, take a seat."

"Mind if I shut the door first?" Davis didn't wait for an answer.

So this was really happening. The eyebrows had sharpened to knives. "I understand. Best to keep my promotion hush hush for now."

"Right." Davis did smile, but he didn't take a chair, just half-sat on the edge of a table. He leaned forward, a palm on each $200 knee. "We know about you and Kyra." Davis quickly shook his head and waved his hands to silence Martin. "In the old days I'da been in here asking cup size and what key she moaned in. Hell I still want to do that, but I don't. Things change. This cannot happen, kid, talent be damned. The people upstairs, whadda they see? X for legal fees. Y in damages. Z in lost revenue. They'll cut you before X happens. That's not a threat; it's a statement of fact."

"What is this, Prizzi's honour?"

"Prizzi's paycheque."

"You *know*, do you? Know's a powerful verb." Martin tilted his head toward the door. "They go home, spouses, I *infer* they're fucking, but do I *know* what really goes on behind closed doors?"

Davis was already standing. "Christ, Martin, this is advertising. We make *know*."

Body-to-body that night he said nothing of the day's tête-à-tête with Davis. Drawers and compartments continued to shut firmly throughout the next day's f-mail and on into another night.

Before a run I loop a strap around my foot to
pull my leg back. The hamstrings are capable
of more stretch than my unassisted leg can

```
give them. What about you?
I have ratchet straps. You have a strong
coffee table.
(Maybe it's the knapsack, black straps in my
hand as I rush in your door.)
```

After, unstrapped, unburdened and very done, she nearly leapt when he pulled a carton of eggs out of the knapsack, stamping one heel and bobbing a knee. "It doesn't take any more gas or time to buy some for you too." Free-range eggs on Saturday. A bag of organic milk on Wednesday night. Before yesterday's threat of poverty he had envied her carless purity. He walked to work, biked downtown for a pint or a new CD. But still, a last-minute movie, groceries.

"If you won't accept any money, I hope you won't say no to a blowjob."

"I'll have to take that one on credit."

Apparently Groucho Marx had been real-estate agent to each of them. Like the company and, Martin now realized, far too many of its employees, he and Kyra were each enraptured by the distillery district, ivy scurrying endlessly over taciturn red brick. Twice a week the air was nutty with the smell of roasting grains, sweet alchemy whispering on the breeze.

Now every fluttering leaf was a spy cam, each old maple a periscope. Neither jog nor drink nor book could dissolve each day's mire of sickening innuendo. The smug grins of office-mates and the drop in invitations from false friends could have smouldered late into sleepless nights save one pure memory solvent. The only thing that could take his mind off the professional, legal and social penalties of fucking Kyra was fucking Kyra. On the floor inside her apartment door. On her kitchen table. Clothes strewn between three of her five rooms every night. The bark of it, the swatting clarity.

Didn't it matter that, unlike every other intern in the history of lip gloss, she was closer to thirty than to twenty? She'd taught English in Hungary, travelled Asia solo for nine months. Learning to scuba dive on Borneo's Sipadan Island, she had scrunched her shoulders and swam up the centre of a helix of swirling jacks, alone in a flashing shape that said *many*. She

71

could budget money, never cried to Mommy or Daddy on the phone and told you quickly and attractively that each of us is already our own ideal lover and that the two of you should cheat on her pussy together.

"These 'feminists' in their $800 pantsuits, why don't they talk to me before assuming I'm your victim? What pleasures are as healthy, as affordable as sex? Fucking zombies whacked out on their libido-dissolving anti-depressants telling each other this crap. And if I am such a victim here, why the hell are they giving *me* the daggers when I walk into the can? What politics. Four thousand years of human civilization, just forty with good birth control and we ruined it in, what, twenty? AIDS was a sideshow. The lab gave us a sex we dismantled in the courtroom. Damages. Damages. Why don't we also measure pleasure? X and Y fucked, and now X is sad. Yeah well while they were fucking X could have been happy, could have soared. Isn't the scale supposed to have two sides? And don't worry lobotomommies, I've found my man."

She was sitting up, had a hand on her cooling back.

"Forget them. We'll stay sore and soaring. Hey, do you mind if I stay? I'll slip off before sunrise."

"I mind if you go, and you know it."

"Well then, can you get the alarm? We can't go mistaking the lark for the nightingale."

"I bite your thumb at them."

Everyone at Click Think chased the soul before the purse. As they made no thing, cured no ailment, and contributed nothing to food, clothing or shelter, they came rich in taste and deep in debt. No-one here was educated in the sciences or engineering or even economics. Getting together for dinner, they were an assembly of the fallen. Authorities on French New Wave cinema and Soviet graphic design dove into the wine list. Ex-painters and atrophying poets knew where their (electronic) car keys were. Brie, the woman to Martin's right, once rappelled naked from a theatre-ceiling in an orgiastic *Mother Courage*. Two decades ago, Davis was in a group show with a young Chuck Close. And then there were the secrets: peed on for video art, wax burns for sculpture, the thinnest of incisions tugged between two photogenic ribs.

Martin knew how much dinner had soothed him, though. Was it what Kyra wanted, too? The year before he started Clicking, (he hasn't yet stooped to saying the year before he started working), the year of his pointless screenplay, he waited tables like these, surfed the derision of gold-card holders who couldn't pronounce Gewürztraminer. But now the weekends in Manhattan, the shoes and convenient things, the lying money.

"The year I was to take Shakespeare," Devon was saying, "the prof insisted on teaching the other guys. What the hell? You have a chance to study a genius and you want to check out the also-rans?"

"Criminal," said Davis. "No-one should be allowed a degree, in anything, without the spear shaker. Study gym if you want, but not without the Richards."

"Absolutely." Martin looked directly at Davis. "You may my glories and my state depose, But not my grieves; still am I king of those."

And so the table ran, a phrase here, a chunk of soliloquy there, the half-remembered traded amongst the half-forgotten. "I am in advertising stepp'd so far returning were as tedious as go over." Glasses chimed repeatedly. Bottles were ordered with a nod. Martin watched Kyra's face emerge from behind a curtain of toasting glasses, saw her look evenly to everyone save him as she invoked the night. "Spread thy close curtain, love-performing night, That the runaway's eyes may wink, and Romeo leap to these arms untalked of and unseen…Something, something…Come night, come, Romeo, come, thou day in night."

"Bravo," a Karen said.

"Shakespeare's best-selling play," claimed Devon.

"On February fifteenth, though, does she actually read it?" Martin asked, exhaling silently.

"Apparently she does," Davis said, closing the night.

From: escapethefire@hotmail.com
Subject: the ape
How 'bout he bursts in while you're doing yoga? You'd already be half naked (and sweaty!!), not to mention all yoged up. (Top

73

and bottom, wear something you don't mind
living without. Don't bathe.) And the mat'll
be handy.
Yes?

From: kyrmeleon@hotmail.com
Subject: yes yog
I'll down that dog, sure.
Mat in living-room, yes, but obviously
she'll run when you burst in. There'll be the
(mandatory!!) chase, the bedroom. (Drag back
to 1.room?)

From: escapethefire@hotmail.com
Subject: rear windows
I'm glad you pretend not to look up at me
when you shut your door and unhook your bra
(then you lock the door, only then). Do you
know which apartment's mine or are you walking around in those bright panties for all of
us, any of us?
I know where your fingers go when you read,
know your a little dope whore.
Signal when you want to know where my telescope is.

From: kyrmeleon@hotmail.com
Subject: you're a
Laughed at 'telescope.' When I get paid
(if???), I'll buy you a Sally Ann trench
coat.

From: escapethefire@hotmail.com
Subject: burst
Hope I'm not bursting the bubble here, but
what about a kinda 'safe' word? Or two? One
for 'stop everything' and one for 'stop that
specific thing' or 'do that but not so hard.'
(I trust you agree 'please' 'stop' and 'no'

are not options).
[Don't worry about the exterior door. I'll
duct tape the latch when I leave tonight.
(New, unopened roll of tape. Gloves.)]

From: kyrmeleon@hotmail.com
Subject: running that
You're the car owner. 'Red' for stop,
'orange' for slow-down (or, race to make it
through if you can.)

Smack, smack, passion never lies. Each day, some days each hour, one of two pairs of hands opened another Russian doll of horny guilt. As significant as the lust, part of the lust, was the shocked gratitude, the fast admiration he felt for her curiosity, her courage. The blessing in her fist, sinner loved along with his hot sin.

The tightness of your grip. The renunciation of your full weight. The closing shove.

Pulse chased pace on the rusting fire escape, his tread pouring along the outside, sucking up the inside. Beyond this quiet metal chute the occasional car passed. Somewhere a dog was barking, a car idling, and he was blubberingly hard. The squeaky section of cat-walk merely sighed. Gagged with mute grey tape, the service door opened noiselessly. Three steps away, her doorknob was doused in fluorescent light. It was the first small thing in his gloved hand.

She did terror well, rolling the closest edge of her body back like another opened door to briefly process the invasion before running down her short hallway. Her breasts swung from a busy chest to the beat of his approaching feet, to the snort of each exhale. Receding down the narrow hall was her spine, the new life-giving tree in his garden. Diving down into a generously low-backed camisole it emerged in her mercifully transparent panties as the crack of her ass, that sculptor's leap from a line to its beautifully marked absence. And it disappeared into her bedroom.

The black-gloved hand he shot at the door would have been crushed if he hadn't followed it with the weight of his shoulder.

She didn't spare the bones of his hand nor did he her shielding arms, her braced legs. Flung deeper into a small room containing no exit other than her barred entrance and consumed by a bed treacherously efficient in its expansive flatness, its unobstructedness, its helpfully low sprawl, she spent seconds glancing hopelessly left then right, searching for an option, a move, when his was clear in front of him.

Again his hand lead. Clothing, extra skin, the warmth we furless few must gather and drape. If she'd been naked, he would have had to lock on wrist or arm and that would have occupied one hand and isolated some of his strength. This occurred to her as a kind of three-image slide-show while her white cotton camisole bunched into his rough black glove, the knee she might have swung into his exposed thigh, the clear punch she'd then have had at his stomach. Instead, chest obediently followed shirt as his right arm pulled her into his shoving left. The underarm and shoulder which so adequately footed her launch to the bed were pinned under a knee in a terrifying blink in time. Pain under became pain on with no memorable interlude. Speed and force continued their spiral as knees, hands and one clawing foot arrested and pried. One rip, two to naked, some remnant balled in her mouth.

His was a reign of touch alone. Any time he stooped for a lick, her ass became a battering ram at the creaking timber of his hips. Only by dropping his chest onto her back could he lick or bite, and that high plains work allowed an uprising in the low countries. Lowering his chest extended his angled legs to a point where hers became stronger. Here in the pin, running through a supply of slaps and kicks made finite by consent and sham, they arrived from opposite directions to a thicket of horrid knowledge. The strength required here was a specific volume of terrifying verticality. His steady pin stretched force out an X-axis of time but did not rise high enough in the Y-axis of severity. The requisite graph wanted incisors, not molars, peaks of terrifying, subjugating force followed by lulls of dull muscle, and neither of them bared fang enough.

By the time of the forced-march back down the hall, the fisted hair was a familiar hat, the arm-bar half a dance. Nearing the strong, compact coffee table and its cache of ratchet straps, their struggles were laughably obliging, arms tugging themselves into place. While the majority of her body was cinched tightly to the table, she enjoyed one uncaptured arm, a mountain rebel which clutched more than it smacked. His unseen licks were deliciously tender, the ministrations of a night-bloom gardener. Each sweep of his large flat hand up or down her back lost two moments of high conductivity as it covered and recovered the snug straps. This tick and tock on the top of her body wed to those below and within.

```
To: escapethefire@hotmail.com
Wow. (I don't look bow-legged in the halls,
do I?) Wow.
```

```
To: kyrmeleon@hotmail.com
Wait, you have legs?
All day I've been lost, beautifully lost.
Oh, I'll be quite late Sat. night. Hal
(Bourne & Elliott's) is having a party.
```

```
To: escapethefire@hotmail.com
Perfect, I'll just re-arrange my cutlery
drawer until you want to cum again.
```

He reached for the phone without a script and without shutting his door. A chagrined, apologetic drone filled his chest and he tried hooking the phone to it, not any argument, knowing key not melody. Her phone rang in each of his ears, as loud in the reluctant receiver as it was three metres down the hall.

"Look, sorry. You've wanted me to paratroop in before. If you'd rather wait until Sunday, I understand."

"I'd rather not wait at all. What's my crime here, having a heart? Of course I don't want you not to go. Why the hell can't we shut a door and make each other feel good?"

"We do, don't we?"

"Sometimes. Thinking about you is wonderful. Thinking about us isn't."

"We've just got to wait it out."

"Right, tend the prison garden."

If her apartment was the prison garden, Hal's party was its mess hall of over-crowded hostility. Martin walked into a high pressure system of hate and notoriety, a thick air with hot spots of sanctimonious ignorance among the hummus dippers and wine glass bobbers. Derision was bought and sold in whirlwinds of rumour and flurries of excommunication. He felt infectious and sharp, a poison cloud, a famed street brawler limber and well-fed in a new hood. "I need to get behind you," he said to a managing consultant over-bronzed with cosmetics who may have already been at the counter, may have backed into it. He poured himself a fishbowl of Shiraz before settling in front of the fridge, a billboard in stainless steel.

Hal himself was the first to address Martin and while this gesture was in no way excluding, his status as host didn't necessarily make it inclusive either. A year ago they'd led competing bids on a Kitchen-Aid contract Martin had eventually won, and he had left the race admiring the reach in Hal's proposal, the shared agreement on a sandy texture and sugary sway they'd mutually described over too many subsequent drinks.

"Well Smart Car, you heard?"

"Grapevines, long-distance plans, I seem to switch one every month."

"I got the nod. Junior Director."

"Remind me to steal some CDs on the way out. I knew I've been wasting time on product when I could have been golfing strategically."

"Playing with fire is what I hear you've been doing."

"We wouldn't be the species we are if somebody hadn't."

A drink was needed from the fridge. The two parted.

On Tuesday he once again put down a buzzing phone receiver and maximized a hotmail window.

```
Don't reply unless you refuse to come.
Otherwise meet me @ Coita Vega @ 7. My treat.
—sMarter
P.S. Black petal shirt??
```

Seeing her through the restaurant window he once again made certain that the two envelope corners were peeking out of each of his jacket pockets.

She accepted and returned his sequence of kisses—cheek, bottom-lip, tongue—with no conspiratorial widening of the eyes, no glance left or right.

"Sorry I'm late. Pure theatricality."

"It's your tab I'm drinking. You look good in the daylight."

"*We* do." He wiggled his chest to emphasize the envelopes. "Are you going to choose one of these or do I go on twirling my pasties all night?"

"No question there. I want what's right."

He signalled a waiter while she withdrew a letter from a previously opened envelope to read "...this letter welcomes you to Bourne and Elliott and is appended by...."

"And the left?" she asked, one hand full.

"I write to terminate my contract and announce my departure from...."

She beamed at him, dropping papered fists onto an unseen tablecloth.

"Let's get champagne," he said.

"And an apartment. Probably a dog."

Roppongi Story
David Whitton

I'd been in Tokyo for six or seven weeks, wandering the streets, drinking in bars, and trying to pick up women with my rudimentary Japanese, when I ran into Mr. Taguchi, the man who changed everything. I met him in Manchester Pub, an expatriate bar in Roppongi. It was a scuzzy place, full of loud Western rock music and stagnant cigarette smoke, but a pint of draught cost only Yen500, so I had no valid complaints. It was a Tuesday night, around eight o'clock. I was sitting at one end of the bar, not talking to or even looking at anyone, paranoid that I might be recognized by one of these expats, and listlessly trying to make sense of a Japanese game show on the overhead television, when Mr. Taguchi dropped, as if from a great height, onto the stool next to me.

"Yes," he said. "Hello. I may buy you drink of beer?"

I was still watching the game show—a man was stuffing bananas down his pants, to much raucous laughter. It took me a second to realize my new neighbour, Mr. Taguchi, was talking to me. "What's that?" I said.

"Yes," he said. "Hello. I may buy you drink of beer in exchange for conversation?"

"No, thanks," I said.

"I may ask one more time?"

I took a look at him. He was stewed, but he seemed harmless enough. He looked like he was here straight from work, a businessman in a white short-sleeved dress shirt and wrinkled black tie.

"All right. Sure. Thank you."

"What have you drink?"

"That one over there. I'm not sure what it's called. The tap on the end."

It was not normally my practice to allow strange men to buy me drinks in a bar, but I was nearly broke. My travellers' cheques were all gone, spent, flown out of my wallet like paper birds.

"My name is Mr. Taguchi," he said, and shook my hand. "And what is your name?"

"Petersen," I lied.

"I may ask, where are you live?" he said.

I toyed with the idea of lying about this, too, but decided simply to leave it vague. "I'm from Canada."

"Canada!" He looked delighted at this. "Montreal," he said.

"That's right."

"London, Ontario."

"Right again."

"African Lion Safari."

"You know your geography."

"Yes," he said. "If you excuse me, I mean no intrusion. I like practise English with English friends."

"I'm happy to have the company."

"I'm happy to have the company, just so," Mr. Taguchi said. He smiled, his black eyes glittering in a mischievous, perceptive kind of way. "I may ask," he said, "what have you do in Japan?"

Now here was an interesting question. What exactly was I doing in Japan? It wasn't at all clear. Hiding? Running? I'd spent most of my days holed up in my filthy little room at the Tengoku Hotel. That was the hiding part. And at nights I walked and drank in bars. That was the running part, I guess. One thing I wasn't doing was deciding. The deciding part was notably absent from my Japanese experience.

"Avoiding lawsuits, mostly."

"Ah, you are avoid lawsuit, therefore you are visit Japan." He nodded, as if this made perfect sense to him.

"Actually, that was sort of a joke."

"Oh." Mr. Taguchi rubbed his chin and threw me a polite smile. "A joke, yes."

Given his overall state of dishevelment, Mr. Taguchi had incongruously perfect hair, thick and black and glossy. He

81

looked in the mirror behind the bar, smoothed his hair with his palm and smiled at himself. I looked like a woodcutter sitting next to him. A fucking fur trader. It'd been a week since I'd shaved, three days since I'd run a comb through my hair. I needed a bath, badly.

"You visit alone?" he asked me.

"Yes."

"This is very strange."

"Well, I'm a strange person."

Mr. Taguchi laughed uproariously at this, slapping the counter and turning pink in the face. "Yes, yes, yes!" he said.

When he'd recovered, he turned to the bartender, an unshaven young man with a ponytail, and said something in Japanese, gesturing with his finger to our coasters. In a moment there was a scotch in front of me, and another in front of Mr. Taguchi.

"I decide for more drink. For new friend."

"Well, okay then," I said. "Fasten your seatbelts."

We stayed at the pub for a couple of hours, give or take. It's hard to say exactly, because we were having so much fun—and had so many scotches. It was the first real conversation I'd had with someone since I'd arrived in Japan. I'd had no idea, until now, how starved I was for some kind of human exchange. For six or seven weeks I'd been walking the streets, avoiding all contact, hoping that somehow, through force of will or something, I might just turn to vapour and float away on the breeze.

"I am 42 years of life," Mr. Taguchi said. "And may I inquire for your own age?"

"I'm 30."

"Ah, yes. You are very young, strong man, with many possibility."

"I suppose I should look at it that way."

"And may I ask, what are you do?"

"You mean, for a living? For a job?"

"For a living. For a job."

"I work at a mutual fund company. Or I did, at least. I was a communications guy. Now I'm...nothing. What about you?"

"Oh, I am very important man," he said, his eyes glittering.

"I am work for government. I am manage of forms and pens."

"Hey. Everyone needs forms and pens."

"My father is work in government and his father is work in government and his father is does the same, and so does his father and his father. All is my family men work in government going many, many years and decades. It is expect in my family. But as my family goes on we grow more strange and more strange, as like you."

"Well," I said, "cheers," and clinked his glass.

He gazed ruminatively at the television set, where a man, dressed like a doctor, held a stethoscope up to a woman's butt. The woman was dressed like a flower. Mr. Taguchi looked suddenly sad.

"Mr. Hirayama is my superior for my job," he said. "He is a very mean man and angry. I hate Mr. Hirayama."

"Uh huh?"

He laughed guiltily. "And I play many trick to my superior."

"Oh yeah? Like what?"

"Example. One time, I drink with Mr. Hirayama after work, and we go to the Manchester Pubs, here, and to other place and other place, and Mr. Hirayama is drink too much, and so he is not go home because wife very angry person. He ask me to take to my home. We go to my home, and he is drink more. But one time, Mr. Hirayama visit bathroom, and so I take..." Mr. Taguchi thought for a second, then pointed toward a beer bottle sitting on the bar.

"Bottle," I said.

"Spot on. And so I take bottle of Mr. Hirayama and..." Here he made a motion as if he were unzipping his fly and urinating into a bottle.

"You pissed into his beer?" I said, incredulous.

"Piss," Mr. Taguchi said. "Piss into his beer."

"Did he drink it?"

"Yes, he come back and he taste drink from beer and say, 'Oh terrible,' and he continue drink."

"He drank the whole thing?"

"He drank the whole thing!"

This was an amazingly malicious act—and I admired him a great deal for it. I thought about all the corporate weasels I used to work for, the ageing jocks and fraternity brothers who'd held such sway over my own life, and who knew it, and who treated me accordingly. Mr. Taguchi was bent double with laughter, tears popping out his eyes. I was laughing right along with him, gleefully, uncontrollably. I hadn't laughed in a long, long time.

When he'd finally calmed himself, and wiped his eyes and blew his nose, Mr. Taguchi turned to the bartender and said something. The bartender scowled and said something back. Mr. Taguchi smiled sheepishly and nodded.

"No more drink," Mr. Taguchi told me. He frowned comically and waggled his index finger in a scolding gesture. "Too many drink."

"No!" I said. "What'll we do?"

He rubbed his chin and stared deep into his scotch glass. He stayed this way for a long time.

"Do you adore girl?"

"Do I.... Well, yes. Yes I do."

"Do you know Shinjuku?"

"I've been there a couple times."

"I go this bar is name Wicked Nun. There are very pretty girl. Very smile girl who are dress up like nun."

"I don't know. That sounds a little...odd."

Mr. Taguchi nodded sagely. "Extreme odd," he said.

"Then what," I said, after a moment's consideration, "are we still doing here?"

And so it was that, half an hour later, we found ourselves in a cold, cavernous hall, surrounded by 500 inebriated business-men, drinking cocktails and chatting up a pretty, round-faced nun who carried a whip.

The nun's name was Reiko, and she was, judging by the way she let him rest his hand on the small of her back, a good friend of Mr. Taguchi's. She took our drink orders.

"May I have..." I scanned the drink list, "the Sublime Enchantment of Angels, please?" The drinks all had names like this: Blood of Virtuous Bliss, Happy Sacred Monk Swallow. During the course of the evening I'd suck back a bunch of them, at Yen10,000 a pop.

"Perfectly decision," Reiko said.

There was something heavenly about Reiko. It was true. She had a benevolent smile and a lovely, smoky voice. But the thing that distinguished her from an actual nun, aside from the whip, was her habit, which was slit up the length of her leg so that you could see her red stockings and garter belt.

As she left to get our drinks, Mr. Taguchi turned to me and said, "Are you marry?"

"Very merry," I said. "More so with each drink."

"No, no," he said, taking a moment to reconsider. "Are you have wife?"

"Oh, I'm sorry…No…I don't have a wife. I'm not married." Which was true: I wasn't married. I didn't have a wife. I did have, not so long ago, a girlfriend. Her name was Angela, and we were together for seven years. Angela was fixated with celebrity weddings and real estate prices, and she possessed not even the crudest understanding of who I really was—but, to be fair, neither did I. Six months ago she discovered herself pregnant with my child. This came as a shock to both of us, though it really shouldn't have, considering our track record with birth control. I reacted inappropriately. I guess I can admit that now: I reacted inappropriately. And then I fled. Not that any of that mattered now; I was pretty sure I didn't have a girlfriend anymore.

"I am marry," he said, showing me the ring on his finger.

"That's great."

"Yes," he said, looking off. "Yes. My wife and I both, we have many secrets from each other and are very playful."

The hall echoed with the sounds of manic carousing: laughter, shouting, singing. It was a mind-fuck to think that outside was Shinjuku, the commercial district, with its pollution, its traffic, its congested sidewalks. It was always daytime in Shinjuku; the giant neon signs bled out into the sky so that the very air glowed. But inside the Wicked Nun it was damp and dim, the only illumination from scores of flickering, wall-mounted candles.

"Is Reiko one of your secrets?"

"Reiko," Mr. Taguchi said, "is exquisitely friend."

A moment later Reiko returned with our drinks. They came in fake gold chalices that took two hands to lift.

"Is taste?" she said.

"Delicious," I said, trying not to grimace. The Sublime Enchantment of Angels tasted a lot like cherry syrup and vodka.

Mr. Taguchi spoke to her in Japanese. She laughed and slapped at his arm. Then she looked over at me, laughed again, and said something to Mr. Taguchi.

"Are you unusual?" she asked me.

"Am I unusual?" I said. "Well, isn't everyone?"

"Do you like unusual things?"

"That depends."

"This is very unusual place."

"I'm beginning to realize that."

"How much do you like unusual things?"

"That also depends."

Reiko came close and gently stroked my head.

"You are very beautiful man," she said. "Your hair are very light."

"Thank you. You're very beautiful yourself."

"Does Mr. Taguchi tell you?" she said. "I am very resemble pet cat. I purred and meow. And I scratch. And I jump from rooftop to rooftop."

"I'd like to see that sometime."

"Sometime I show to you."

In this manner the night progressed. And it was turning out to be one of the greatest nights of my life. Reiko would come around, bring us our mystery cocktails, and whisper strange and suggestive things in my ear. Mr. Taguchi said, "Reiko is love you. She is sex with you very much." Which struck me as terrific news, because I was sex with her very much, too. But it never happened. It never happened because I couldn't get her phone number. And I couldn't get her phone number because we got tossed out of the bar. In his compromised state, Mr. Taguchi had said something to one of the passing nuns, and said nun had taken offence, and presently two muscular, shirtless men came along to escort us to the street. At least that's as far as I was able to piece it together. My memories of that part of the evening are out of focus and scrambled together. All I know for sure is that at two in the morning we were out on the gaudy Shinjuku street—and I was out of luck.

86

"Where are we go now?" Mr. Taguchi said. This was more of a rhetorical question; he wasn't asking me.

"I think I should probably just wander back to my hotel-room and crash," I told him.

"No, no, no. You accompany my place. Is no question. My home take five minute to travel."

"I appreciate"—it was hard to get this word out, I was slurring so badly—"the offer, but I really, really, really, really need to sleep."

"One more drink," Mr. Taguchi said. "For friendship."

I looked at Mr. Taguchi, wobbling proudly in the neon glare. He looked battered, he looked blighted, but his hair, as usual, was flawless. Friendship, he said. This man was my friend. He was my friend.

"Okay," I said. "Let's do it. Let's go have a drink."

Mr. Taguchi lived in a tiny, spotless unit on the twenty-seventh floor of a high-rise apartment tower. Contrary to his claim, it didn't take us five minutes to get there; it took us five minutes to cab it to the train station—and then it took us an hour or more by train, because his building was located somewhere in the middle of a vast Tokyo suburb.

We stepped into his front hall. Mr. Taguchi flipped on a bright white light, pressed a finger to his lips for me to be quiet, then slipped off his slip-on shoes and tiptoed into the living-room.

Not a thing was out of place in here—besides Mr. Taguchi and me, that is. Magazines were stacked precisely on the shiny beech coffee table. Pillows sat beautifully on the low blue sofa. Mr. Taguchi got me a beer from the kitchen, which was not eas-ily distinguishable from the living-room and the dining-room, and motioned for me to sit while he snuck into the bedroom to check on his wife.

In less than a minute he was out again, his wife beside him.

"Mr. Petersen," he said, "please meet my wife, is name Mrs. Taguchi."

"Pleasure to meet you," I said.

Mrs. Taguchi was wearing just a filmy yellow nightdress, and her hair was bed-messy, but she looked happy enough to be awake at four in the morning.

"Very glad to meet," she said. "You are handsome man."

"Thank you very much. That's very kind."

"Please enjoy our home. Stay for long since needed."

She excused herself and retreated back into the bedroom with her husband. While they were in there, I took the opportunity to check out my reflection in the sliding glass door that led out onto the balcony. What I saw there didn't look like me. I looked like a debauched ghost. I looked like vapour. I wanted to apologize to Mrs. Taguchi, explain that I didn't usually look this way.

Mr. Taguchi came in now and took a seat on the couch beside me.

"My wife is 34 years of life," he said.

"She looks much younger than that."

"Yes." Mr. Taguchi picked up his beer. "We are very want children; however, my wife is foul womb."

"I...I'm sorry to hear that."

Mr. Taguchi patted my knee. He looked curiously cheerful.

"Have you notice," he said. "Is something wrong with me?"

"Is something wrong with you?"

"Yes." He was smiling at me.

Oh, God, I thought, here it comes. I was half-expecting something like this. My new friend Mr. Taguchi was about to make a pass at me. Either that or involve me in some weird sex thing with his patient, sleepy wife. Not that I was averse to weird sex things, but this was just too much. This was just too much for one night.

Mr. Taguchi stood up. He beckoned for me to stand up, too.

"I want is confess."

Still grinning, he lifted his hands to his head and made odd tugging motions at his hair. There was a loud pop. Then a second. Then a third and a fourth.

With glittering eyes, Mr. Taguchi lifted the hair off his head like it was a motorcycle helmet, and laid it on the coffee table, on top of the magazines. He let out a contented sigh and ran a hand over his pale, shiny head. He was almost entirely bald.

"Wow," I said, dropping back down onto the sofa. "That's...that's amazing. I would never have known." It was true. I was stunned, honestly stunned. It had never occurred to me that his hair might not be real.

"Hair is snap on. Is excellent method." He lowered his head for me to admire. Surgical steel buttons had been implanted into the sides of his skull. "Mrs. Taguchi is very much like full hair. And so...." He lifted his hair off the magazines and dropped it into my lap.

"That," I declared, "is the finest hairpiece in the history of hairpieces."

Mr. Taguchi looked pleased. "My need is confess," he said. "And so here now I confess."

Much later, when I knew him better, I wondered if this had been an act of provocation, if Mr. Taguchi had orchestrated his little confession because he knew there was something I wasn't revealing myself. If it was, it worked. When I heard those snaps coming off, when I saw the hair float away, everything came into focus—the sky opened up and the white light came pouring through. I saw, with an almost premonitory clarity, a picture of my new life. I'd find a new girlfriend, I'd learn her language, I'd get some kind of job, possibly involving forms and pens—and, above all, I would never, ever live more than a train ride away from the Taguchis. All I had to do was come clean.

"My name isn't Petersen," I told him. "My name is Maltman."

Mr. Taguchi looked ecstatic. "Ah," he said. "Wait for minute. I pouring special drink is vodka from Malaysia. One must be careful if consume."

We went out onto the balcony with our new drinks, which tasted not unlike gasoline, and sat in sky-blue plastic patio chairs, and let the dark morning air wash over us.

I told him how I didn't think I was cut out for the Western hemisphere. I told him about my job in corporate communications, and how, six or seven weeks ago, I forfeited it when I sent out a company-wide e-mail that read: "Dear assholes, You're all a bunch of stinking corporate swine, and you can all go fuck each other." I told him about my girlfriend, Angela, and how she didn't understand me, and how I got her pregnant, and how, when I found out she was pregnant, I reacted inappropriately. I told him how, after I'd found out, I got drunk, ran into her little sister, Blair, an angry and comely young philosophy student, at a local rock club, and took her home and seduced her. I told him how maybe it was the other way around, how maybe she seduced me. I told him how we continued to seduce each other for the next three months, until, for reasons I hadn't fully come to grips with, I booked a flight to Japan—and disappeared. I told him I thought maybe I wouldn't be going back anytime soon.

I spilled, and Mr. Taguchi listened. He smiled sympathetically, said little, and put his hand on my knee. Two months ago, where was I? Sitting in the boardroom of an office tower, staring longingly out the windows. Now here I was, eleven time zones away, on the twenty-seventh floor of an apartment tower, sipping scary Malaysian vodka with a man who, twelve hours earlier, had been a stranger, a man who tortured his boss for sport, a man with bolts fused into the bones of his head. This man, he knew how to live a life. I could learn things from a man like this. We sat together silently, watching the dawn light swell up in the eastern sky and spill across the city, so that all the rooftops of Tokyo turned purple.

Moments before we passed out, both of us, right there on the balcony, Mr. Taguchi turned to me, his head bobbing, his eyelids heavy.

"This area are very, very superb and also very peculiar," he said, "full of wretched sorrow and beautiful splendour. Is difficult to wonder. Three time, yes, but is false visions? No, no, no, no. In travel with extreme excitement. Do you say?"

"Yes," I said. Maybe it was the vodka, maybe the terrifying height, but, for a couple of fugitive moments, Mr. Taguchi's words made absolute sense. "Yes, I think I do. Yes. I know exactly what you're saying." It was almost daylight; you could see the early morning traffic snaking through the streets far below. "I know exactly what you're saying, and I couldn't agree more."

Six Million Million Miles

Michael Bryson

All of a sudden Patrick was nearly 40. Yes, he'd noticed birthdays piling up, but it took his doctor to impress upon him the meaning of numbers.

Patrick told his buddy Phil, "The doc said I should see a nutritionist, change my diet, take calcium pills for my teeth and bones. He said he needed to test my blood for LDLs and HDLs. Of course he said, 'Stop the smokes and moderate the drinking,' but I was expecting that." What he wasn't expecting: A finger up the butt.

Phil said, "Wha?"

"A finger up the butt, to test the colon, I think."

"The colon, eh? What's that do?"

"I don't know, but it can kill you if it goes off."

"I guess so," said Phil, who was already 41, though he hadn't been in a doctor's office in ten years and wasn't about to go now, whatever Patrick said.

It was three minutes past three on a Saturday afternoon in May. Phil had an ex-wife and two small children in Vancouver he hadn't seen in five years. He had a 28-year-old girlfriend, Debbie, who lived with her parents and slept with him on Saturdays and Wednesdays. Her father was dying. Her father had been dying all of the time Phil had known her, which was going on three years. He wanted to marry her because he wanted to be married. He wanted a home again with a woman in it. He had to wait for the old man to die. It wasn't something he'd ever heard about, a marriage contingent upon a death.

They were sitting on Patrick's couch, watching curling. Patrick and Phil had a business venture, but it was still in the "idea phase." That's what Patrick told everyone who asked.

"We're still working out the details." It was an idea they'd first had years earlier, before the dot-coms collapsed.

"What do people need?" Phil said one day. "That's how you make money, by selling people what they need, what they can't live without."

"Food," Patrick said. "Heat, shelter, love." He wasn't sure about love.

Phil was on a different wavelength.

"Office supplies," he said. "You sell a pen for a dollar that costs pennies to make. We'll make a killing."

They tried to register www.officesupplies.com, but it had already been taken.

"The best laid plans of mice and men," Patrick said, but Phil demurred.

"We'll make it work."

Patrick wanted to find a way to make money by making art. He'd started gluing things together to create new things. Toothbrushes and staplers. Matchbooks and condoms. Playing cards and plastic figurines. He had no idea what any of it meant, but he kind of enjoyed the process. Art had no place on Maslow's Hierarchy of Needs, unless it fell under "self-fulfillment."

Patrick thought Maslow would have associated the need with the consumer not the producer. Gluing together random objects or lacing together papier mâché might make one feel good, but as Auden said, "Poetry makes nothing happen."

Today, it was the women who were curling.

Phil said, "If you were a woman, would you wear makeup to the rink?"

"I'd wear makeup if I knew I was going to be on TV."

"Good point." One of the reasons Phil broke up with his wife was because she stopped shaving her legs. Okay, not true. He broke up with his wife because they fought all of the time. One of the things they fought about was her legs. Or his "expecta-tions." The subject of their fights changed depending on who you talked to about it. She thought Phil needed to revise his expectations, and he thought she needed to shave her legs.

Outside, it rained heavily. They were waiting for JayCee to arrive. JayCee was Patrick's ex. She taught kindergarten in the suburbs. She was 42, sometimes looked 30 and sometimes looked 50. They'd met at a dinner party held by mutual friends two years ago. For past three months, JayCee had found an excuse to skip out on all of their dates. She didn't like the city, she hated the commute, she was over-worked and needed a quiet day alone. So Patrick started to call her his ex. Not that they had ever been a couple. Not really.

"It's a post-structuralist romance," he told Phil, who had no idea what he was talking about.

Patrick's doctor told him he was good for another 10,000 miles. "But come back and see me next year." Patrick imagined his life like a pancake. Flat, doughy. Where was the maple syrup? Where was the fruit, the whipped cream?

Suddenly, the television shook on its stand and the air filled with the sound of a large explosion.

Patrick thought, "A bomb!"

Phil jumped up from the couch and ran out to Patrick's balcony.

"Flames!" he said, pointing two streets over. Soon they heard sirens from firetrucks. A plume of black smoke lifted into the sky.

Patrick said, "Life is a strange and multi-glorious thing, isn't it?"

"Just one step from Paradise," Phil said.

The rain was now like a sheet of water. They stood away from the railing of the balcony to avoid getting soaked. Patrick remembered something Phil had said to him when they'd first met: "Just do the best you can. You can't do any better than that." Even if his best was 2 + 2 = 3. The words had gone straight to his heart. Why was he thinking of them now?

The wind was picking up. Two streets over, the flames from the explosion leaped higher. "I'm going inside," Patrick said. There had been women once. In his twenties, Patrick had played guitar, travelled the country. He spent four years on buses and trains, in vans and motels. He'd been all motion, all movement. All process with no end in sight. The arc of his life had seemed different then. Each high made the downs bearable. The future, he'd thought: Where stasis lay. Once, there had been three girl-friends in three provinces. He'd thought, "One of these women, surely, will be my wife." But they had each wanted him as an occasional friend. Back then, he'd looked forward and seen a landing pad. The arc had been rising, pointed upwards in an optimistic spiral. But the landing pad had not been forward and up; it had been backward and down. A crash pad.

"Illusions are made for shattering," he'd said to JayCee, mimicking Nancy Sinatra. JayCee worked with four- and five-year-olds. She knew about hope. She knew about limits.

"Potential is earned," she told Patrick, who felt for her suddenly all warm and loving.

The buzzer went off.

"She's here," Patrick yelled to Phil. He walked across the apartment to buzz down and let JayCee into the building. Phil came in from the balcony.

"There's three houses on fire down there," he said.

"What was that?" Patrick asked. He'd gone into the kitchen.

"There's three houses on fire down there," Phil said.

Patrick said, "Oh, shit. Really? Lots of firetrucks, too?"

"About eight or ten."

Patrick uncorked a bottle of wine and laid out two baguettes on the kitchen table. He poured himself a glass.

"You should invite Debbie over," he said to Phil. "We should all just stay in tonight. Stay in and talk. Give her a call. See what she says. I haven't seen her in ages."

Phil nodded. He went to get his cell phone.

There was a knock on the door.

"About six million million miles," Patrick heard someone say when he opened it. JayCee stood there smiling. She gripped him and kissed him on the cheek. Beside her, a man shook water off of an umbrella.

JayCee said, "Patrick, this is Jason."

The man reached out to shake Patrick's hand. Patrick shook it.

"What's six million million miles?" he asked.

JayCee brushed past him into the apartment. "A light year. The amount of distance light travels in a year." JayCee embraced Phil and kissed him on the cheek. "Phil, this is Jason. Jason, Phil." The two men shook hands. They were all in the apartment now. Patrick closed the door.

"I'll take some of that," JayCee said, pointing to Patrick's wine glass. "Some for Jason, too. Right Jason?"

The man nodded. "That would be terrific."

"How far is the sun from the earth?" Patrick mumbled. "How far are we from each other?" He went to the kitchen to fetch glasses and wine.

"Home is elsewhere," Jason was saying when Patrick returned with the wine. Jason was telling a story about one of his co-workers, a Russian Jew who'd left the Soviet Union for Israel, then come to Canada two years later.

"Immigration is a disaster," Jason said.

This was apparently the Russian man's thoughts. His life had been torn asunder. He was raising a daughter, taking her to chess tournaments. He had a library with 10,000 Russian books. "Ten per cent of what he had in Russia." His wife had a PhD and worked at IBM.

"They're desperately lonely people," JayCee said. "Lonely but not unhappy. They have that wonderful, dark, Russian sense of humour. You know, *life is bleak*, but they laugh a lot. They're terribly homesick, but they would never go back. They see their situation as immeasurably better and also not good."

Jason had taken her over to their house. Patrick saw she was sitting next to him on the couch. He wasn't sure he'd ever seen her so happy.

"There's a fire outside," he said. "There was a large explosion, and now there are three houses on fire. Phil and I were watching from the balcony. There's eight firetrucks. It's a huge disaster."

They all looked at him.

JayCee asked, "Is Debbie coming?"

Phil nodded. "She's coming. I called her. She'll be here in a bit."

Suddenly, there was another large *boom!* They jumped up and followed Patrick to the balcony. The rain was still heavy. Water dripped on Patrick's head from the balcony above. Where one of the burning houses once stood, a blue flame shot twenty metres into the air. From the street below, they could hear people screaming. Blue and red lights from emergency vehicles flashed off nearby buildings. They could see firemen scrambling and police officers stringing up yellow tape and pushing back spectators clutching umbrellas.

"I'm getting wet. I'm going inside," JayCee said.

Jason and Phil followed her.

Patrick wiped the water off his head and found a spot on the balcony where he could stay reasonably dry. He'd brought his wine glass with him. He took a sip. He could hear the rest of them inside, picking up their conversation. Jason was saying, "The Beatles deconstructed the pop song. They started writing verse, verse, chorus, verse, then they broke the mould and improvised all kinds of arrangements. U2 followed a similar trajectory—" Patrick crossed his arms against his chest. He could see three more firetrucks approaching the blue flame. The wind changed direction and blew a spray of water across his face. He lifted his shirt and wiped it off, then he went inside.

What happened next was more of the same. Debbie arrived. Patrick refilled wine glasses. They ordered pizza and discussed the possibility of playing Monopoly or Risk. Phil and Debbie had an argument about how to make real Italian spaghetti. JayCee kept touching Jason on the knee. Patrick kept his eyes open and knew things were being said that weren't being talked about. He excused himself to do the dishes, tidy up the kitchen. Outside, the blue flame went out. The rain stopped. The sun went down. The firetrucks, the police officers and the spectators went home. The next day the newspapers said a miracle happened. A gas explosion blew one house off of its foundation. Two others burned to the ground. No-one died. Patrick spent the night on the couch. He woke up hungover.

Most Wanted

Vivette J. Kady

Maddox didn't bother trying to stop his wife when she left him three months ago. He figured only a lunatic would imagine he could compete with Jesus.

"That's it? You're not even gonna try and make me stay?" Francie asked after he'd carried some of her stuff out to a van driven by a pale, plump, youngish woman named Hannah, one of the Born-Agains from the commune Francie moved to. Francie didn't take much with her—most things she'd boxed and tagged for charity.

Maddox shrugged. "Waste of time."

Hannah was standing tactfully off to the side with a smile on her blanched face, apparently transfixed by a squirrel's enthusiastic trapeze act. Her hands were clasped behind her back and every so often she'd rise up on tiptoes. She was humming something, her whole demeanour radiating righteousness, and Maddox half-expected her to burst into sudden full-throated song—Julie Andrews maybe, or a rollicking gospel number. Or else to levitate, her holy doughboy body hovering miraculously a few feet off the ground. He felt a dangerous hostility toward her.

Francie searched his face with her moist martyr-eyes. "You could've at least *tried*," she said.

Hannah's farewell handshake was about as limp and clammy as seaweed. Francie hugged him hard and promised to pray for him.

"Go ahead," Maddox said, "if it makes you feel good." He opened the passenger door for her and gave the side of the van, which sported a predictable array of banal religious slogans, a couple of good-natured thumps as it pulled away. Much as one

97

might slap the rump of a horse or a cow, he thought, or Hannah's ample ass. He waved them out of sight, aware as he did so that he was displaying admirable maturity and restraint through all this—hell, *grace* even—then he went inside, swallowed a Percodan (left over from Francie's gum surgery), lay down on the bed with his boots on and stared up at the ceiling for an hour or so. When he got up, he wandered into the kitchen, grabbed a beer and started flinging steak knives at the cross-stitched sampler Francie had embroidered and hung on the wall between the fridge and the stove. "In the House of the Righteous Is Much Treasure," the sampler proclaimed. There was another sampler in the bedroom, nailed slap-bang over the marital bed. "Draw Nigh to God and He Will Draw Nigh to You," that one said, which Maddox found at least as effective as a cold shower.

The phone rang. It was Francie. He could tell she'd been crying. "What are you doing?" she asked.

"Fucking up the wall," he answered, squinting at the gouged drywall where a knife had struck.

"I worry about you," she told him.

He knew this would be a good moment to say, "I miss you already. Please come home," or something to that effect. Time to lay on the tenderness—she was already weepy; he was halfway there.

"The fuck you do," is what Maddox said, hanging up the phone and aiming another steak knife at the sampler. From now on he'd keep score—twenty points for each embroidered letter.

Sure Signs of a Meltdown:
1. Using sampler as a dartboard.

In the three months since then, Maddox has gained thirteen pounds. He's also got himself a dog and a new Fender Stratocaster. He's making a mental list at the moment, Gained versus Lost (in between channel surfing and scarfing down nachos, the dog snoozing and drooling beside him on the couch). Thus far all he's come up with for Lost is Francie's awesome hash brownies. Double chocolate chip, moist and chewy, although he can't remember when last she baked them. Maddox has lately developed the habit of near-compulsive list-making—Twenty All-Time Favourite Movies; Best Blues Albums; Top Ten Reasons Not to Move to Budapest; Foods to Request on Death Row (the brownies top that list too); Five Most Wanted (he's already got the guitar and the dog, but still covets the BMW GS 1150 Adventure motorbike, a 50-inch plasma TV and Halle Berry). He adds sex to Lost, then changes his mind. He needs to join a gym.

Maddox finds Francie's evangelical zeal downright obnoxious. Fact is, she became a major drag after her lightning-bolt conversion. She used to be fun, she'd been wild, she was an ex-*groupie* for Chrissakes (one or two of INXS, most of Guns N' Roses and a handful of roadies, as far as he knows) and then all of a sudden there she was organizing revival meetings and singing hymns on street corners while handing out pamphlets urging redemption. She approached religion with the same enthusiasm she'd previously directed to aromatherapy and Tantric sex, developing self-righteousness and a ridiculously serene *glow.* Night after night he'd find her sitting there glowing away piously with the New Testament open on her lap as gospel-era Dylan or the Mighty Clouds of Joy trumpeted through the house.

And yet Maddox can't shake the belief that he's largely responsible for her transformation. Unintentionally so, but responsible nevertheless.

What happened was this: two years ago he and Francie were living in a soon-to-be-condemned loft on the top floor of a disused zipper factory. A pizza delivery guy rang the doorbell one evening while Maddox was playing his electric guitar. The building was ancient, the wiring faulty, and when Maddox stopped strumming long enough to turn the metal doorknob with his right hand (his fretting hand still holding a chord on the neck of the guitar), he became part of the circuit and fried himself. Francie told him later that the pizza delivery guy was crawling around the floor frantically, using the broom to tug at every cord in sight. She straddled Maddox's waist, pounded his chest with her small fists and screamed at him. That's when the praying started. Until the paramedics arrived, she gave Maddox mouth-to-mouth, and each time she lifted her head to take another breath she somehow managed to keep on screaming at him and pleading and bargaining with God. She was still praying hours later while he lay recuperating in a hospital bed. Whenever Maddox opened his eyes Francie was at his side, eyes squeezed shut and lips barely moving as she whispered her soft prayers. Her childlike hand fluttered over his bandage, coming to rest on it briefly from time to time, light as a hummingbird.

"Give it a rest," he mumbled a couple of times, but if she heard she took no notice.

Maddox came away from this close call with the strings of a Stratocaster forever branded in deep grooves across the fingers of his left hand, and Francie came away with Religion.

Comparisons to Jesus:
1. I too am no slouch as a carpenter.
2. I once had a beard (okay, a goatee. For six weeks max. But still).
3. Soulful eyes.

The dog, Duane, just about breaks Maddox's heart. He's a three-legged mutt Maddox rescued from the pound shortly after Francie's departure. Duane lost his left foreleg in an incident of abuse too terrible to contemplate—something involving an apartment building's garbage chute—and he has at least one metal pin in his hip and/or spine. The dog-adoption lady at the pound told Maddox the damage wasn't only physical. "The poor thing still gets depressed. Bless him," she sighed, and Maddox had to suppress an intense urge to wrap his arms around this matronly woman who blessed poor mutts like Duane, even though her mutt-blessing might indicate religious tendencies that would normally piss him off. But it isn't Duane's occasional bouts of depression that bother Maddox (episodes in which the dog just sits there, bracing himself on his remaining foreleg and staring morosely at the ground for unbelievably long periods) so much as the flip side—the dog's irrational *optimism* in the face of such a raw deal. It's the way he hobbles eagerly after squirrels or Frisbees or non-disabled dogs in the park, all waggling excitement to begin with until he finally stops and quivers, no doubt realizing there's no way he'll ever be coordinated or fast enough to get by in this world, but thumping his stoic tail nevertheless and grinning pathetically as if to console Maddox; or the way he loses his balance from time to time and topples over, righting himself with a sneeze and a sheepish tilt of the head. Even thinking about these things is enough to make Maddox want to weep.

But Maddox is not above using the sorry creature as a magnet for tenderhearted women. They look stricken when they first see Duane, then they crouch and slap their knees, cooing, "Aw! Come over here," and Maddox gives them small sad smiles and thinks, *Bingo!*

His latest job—built-in entertainment and shelving units of cherry and curly maple, which he started to make a couple of days ago for a droopy little fashionista whose name escapes him—came from just such an encounter. The fashionista (Paula? Sheila? Lauren?) wore a miniskirt and stiletto-heeled knee-high boots for a walk in the park with her skittish borzoi. "Maddox?" she'd murmured while scratching poor Duane's ears with her tastefully manicured fingernails. She was gazing at Maddox with such fierce sincerity she looked almost cross-eyed. "Is that your first name?" The fashionista, who's an entertainment lawyer, is slouch-shouldered with seal-sleek hair and a narrow face. She has the weird pointed intensity of a long-necked exotic bird—an ibis or emu, or maybe an ostrich. "I'm a total design maniac. Honestly, I *worship* great design," she announced when she hired him, and Maddox finds it amusing that her hugely expensive new midtown condo is actually an eighth of a renovated church. Standing in the cathedral-ceilinged living-room, with mid-afternoon light flashing through the clerestory windows, Maddox asked what sort of look she was after for the wall units. Photographs of his work were spread across the coffee table, alongside lacquered bowls filled with wasabi rice crackers and piri-piri root chips and organic tapenade. Paula/Sheila/Lauren was wearing low-slung jeans and a back-baring suede halter-top that Maddox found mildly arousing. "Something high end," she replied, frowning as she gazed at the empty wall. "Different, but classy." She looked at Maddox and nodded earnestly. "I've got a lot of faith in you. Really. Just go ahead and knock me out with the design." Her thin arms were held at her sides like snapped wings. *Peck, peck*, he thought, and nodded back.

As if Maddox's life weren't enough for her, Francie became hell-bent on saving his soul as well. "Listen. Whatever gets you through the night, I don't care. Just count me out," he told her, but it did no good.

Shortly before she left, she presented him with a list of conditions. On top of the page was written *Wish List*, and underneath that Francie had listed about a dozen items in her loopy script.

"What the hell is this?"

"My wish list," she replied quietly, nodding for emphasis. "Things I want you to do. To see if we can put us back together again."

It was a pitiful list. As Maddox recalls, it went something like this:

1. Come to church, at least on Sundays.
2. Attend revival meetings, once a month minimum.
3. Stop getting wasted.
4. Cut the blasphemy.
5. Quit belittling me about my faith,

and so on. There was also

11. Chew properly,

which had nothing to do with her religious fervour—she just hated the way he ate.

"Jesus. Don't you think this is a bit much?" Maddox waved the piece of paper in front of Francie's nose. "I mean, how about a little give and take here, a little tit for tat? What do you say we trade?"

Her face tightened. "Trade?"

"Yeah. Let's do a little exchange. Like, say, a revival meeting for a couple of blowjobs. Or three. Hell, it's worth at *least* three."

Francie just sat there staring at the floor and looking as if she might cry. Maddox reached for her fist but she pulled it away. "Christ," he said, not unkindly. "What the hell has happened to you?"

Finally she looked up at him and in a tired voice said, "Just so you know. This stuff is not negotiable."

The fashionista, who named her borzoi Manolo, after the shoe designer, drew a blank on Duane. "Who?" she asked in her sharp, birdlike way, then shrugged dismissively when Maddox explained. "I'm not really big on guitarists," she told him.

Francie, on the other hand, never missed a beat. Her taste in music might have spiralled embarrassingly south lately (Mercy Me? Amy Grant, for Chrissakes?) but when Maddox told her about his new three-legged pal she said, "Duane, huh. So you named your dog after an Allman brother?"

This was during one of their late-night phone calls. At first it was always Francie who did the calling. "Hey, Francie!" Maddox would say. "How's it going in zombie land?" She whispered so she wouldn't wake the other Born-Agains. "You could call me too sometimes, you know. It wouldn't kill you."

Maddox began calling every now and then when he couldn't find things—documents, box-cutters, spare chequebooks. The first time he called he was put on hold for about five minutes. Instead of Muzak, he had to listen to a recording of a jarringly chirpy woman's voice: "These beautiful pewter crown-of-thorns lapel pins and pendants are a one-time offer. The pendants are on an attractive leather thong and both pieces come with a handy satin drawstring pouch for storage. They're available for purchase at the church office for $29.99 each, or from our website at soulredemption.com. New witness kits are also now available at the office, and Trucker Dan is presently transporting these kits to our brethren across the country. Let us all give thanks and pray for their safe delivery, and for a blessed journey for Trucker Dan. The annual bake sale and bazaar takes place on the fifteenth...."

"Hello?" Francie sounded worried.

"Hi. So did you get your crown-of-thorns necklace yet?"

"My what?"

"Never mind. Where's the plant spray? There's an infestation here."

"Should be in the laundry cupboard. Behind the shoe polish.

An infestation?"

"Yep. A nasty one. Aphids."

"Uh-oh. You're not going to kill them, are you?"

He'd forgotten about Thou Shalt Not Kill, Not Even Aphids. "Hell no, I'm just planning to stun them with a light mist of insecticide."

There was silence on the other end of the line.

"Don't worry, I'll bless them first. Let them say their prayers and save their little souls before they buy the farm. They'll all go straight to aphid heaven, I promise. Unless I can find some ants real quick."

"You lost me."

"They herd them."

"What are you talking about?"

"Ants. They love aphids. Aphids are ant cows."

"You're making this up."

"No, I'm not. Aphids give off some kind of secretion the ants go crazy for. They corral them, take them back to the ant heap and milk them. I'm not kidding. They stroke them and sweet-talk them and the aphids give them what they want. It's a beautiful thing."

"I don't know, Maddox. Where do you *get* this stuff?"

"Hey, listen to this," he said casually, as if he'd just thought of it, reaching for his acoustic guitar and placing the phone in front of him so she could hear him play something new.

Aside from Francie's irritating habit of quoting from the Scriptures, Maddox has come to realize he actually looks forward to her calls. He is comforted by the easy intimacy they've settled into on the phone, and besides, her inane jabber about abounding love and light and miracles works better than any sleeping pill. He listens to her go on and on and feels the tightness in his jaw dissolve with the slow rise and fall of her voice.

"Pastor Jenkins went on a rampage this morning," she'll whisper as she brings him up to speed on commune gossip and fills him in on the day-to-day stuff—the veggie prep and book-keeping and admin for which they pay her diddly squat ("Yeah, but there's really nothing I need," Francie, who went and shut down her aromatherapy practice when she moved out, insists); the hours of Bible study; the sing-alongs and suppers and the histrionics of Pastor Jenkins, who scares his flock witless with his palsied rants about a Hell so dark you couldn't see your own hand in front of your face, so hot your flayed flesh would sizzle and curl from your blistered bones in festering strips, whereupon the faithful moan and sob and shout their Glad Amens and Hallelujahs and Praise the Lords and the newly saved flop down wailing and babbling, their dripping noses pressed to the carpet.

"Sounds pretty dramatic."

"Oh, you have *no* idea."

One evening she was giving him the lowdown on her evangelical excursions with the rest of the door-to-door devout. "Witnessing and Inviting," she called it, telling him they fan out and work a neighbourhood in pairs. Her Witnessing and Inviting partner is the pale and ample-assed Hannah.

He said, "God salesmen, that's what you are."

Her enthusiastic response surprised him: "That's it!"

"Remember Balsam Avenue?" he said. "Those Jehovah's Witnesses?"

A couple of stiff-hipped Watchtower-proffering women had shown up one too many Saturday mornings—ridiculously early, as always—at the place they were renting five or six years ago. This time he and Francie were ready for them. They waited until the unsuspecting pair came trundling up the front walk, then dropped their jeans and mooned the Witnesses, yelling, "Hey, ladies, witness *this!*" as they shoved their bare asses up against the screen door. They'd whooped and gasped with laughter while the women retreated in hasty slack-jawed horror, cheeks flapping, elbows and copies of the Watchtower flying every which way.

"Bet they never knew they could run so fast."

"Yeah, well," she said after a long pause. "There's a whole lot of things I'm not exactly proud of."

"I don't know, Francie. Why couldn't you just become a Unitarian, or a run-of-the mill Methodist or something? Why does everything have to be so goddam *extreme?*"

What I really miss about Francie:

1. That incredible thing she used to do with her tongue.

2. How she twitches in her sleep like a kid.

3. The way she plays with her hair while she reads, even the Bible.

4. All those years she'd listen to "Stairway to Heaven" first thing in the morning.

Lately Maddox has been telling Francie about the fashionista, hoping to make her jealous.

"You would not believe this woman's condo," he said.

"'Unless the Lord builds the house, they labour in vain who build it,'" was her smug response.

He has also mentioned Francie to the fashionista. Yesterday morning, over a mochaccino in her new state-of-the-art kitchen, it slipped out before he could stop himself. "My wife left me. Actually, not that long ago," he said, raising his eyebrows and biting the corner of his lower lip.

"God. That's terrible."

"Yep. Three months ago. She left me for Jesus, you believe that?" He gave a little snorting laugh. "I mean, talk about being out of my league."

"Boy," she said slowly, as if giving this information serious thought.

There was no stopping him once he got started. He held up his scarred fingers. "You see these?"

"Oh wow." She squinted at the skin grafts and sucked in air with what appeared to be genuine sympathy, but since her default expression was genuine sympathy he couldn't be certain.

He told her about his near-electrocution, about Francie's shocking transformation, about the subsequent bitter wrangling for his soul. He even told her about Francie's hash brownies.

"Now there I can help you," the fashionista said. "There's a guy who makes these unbelievable biscotti. I'm talking *incredible*. Like, all you need is a quarter—a whole one would do you in." She patted his damaged hand. "Tell you what. If you come to my party tonight, I'll order some, just for you." Maddox started to make an excuse, but she said, "Come on, it's my birthday."

She was flirting with him, he realized, in her weird birdlike way. "Really? Happy birthday," he drawled, grinning at her.

"Oh, thank you," she said coyly, then snared him with her ultra-sincere gaze. "It's no big deal, but you know, there's just so much horrible stuff going on in the world. We have to celebrate every chance we get. No really, I truly believe that. This place isn't finished yet but what the heck. It'll be very low key, just some good friends. And hey, it's Friday night. Please come."

He showed up late, bearing a bromeliad, which had seemed perfect for her with its single bizarre pink flower spiking from an improbably thin stem.

"Aw. That is so *sweet*," she gushed, air-pecking both his cheeks and placing the plant on the hallstand with her other gifts. Apparently all except his were lavishly wrapped. "Come get a drink and meet everyone. Everyone, this is Maddox. He makes *great* furniture." She leaned in close and whispered conspiratorially, "Ta da! See? Biscotti." She pointed to a plate on a side table. "I had to cut them up so people don't get totally wasted. Butchered them a bit but hey, they taste the same. They take a while to kick in but they're *so good*. Ooh, Maddox, here, meet Bill, my designer. He's brilliant. You both are, you're both brilliant. You guys should talk."

Maddox refrained from sharing his theory on interior designers, which is that they are entirely superfluous (his logic being as follows: your space should reflect your own personality, therefore unless you're willing to totally negate yourself and live inside someone else's personality, you should not hire one, ever). "How's it going," he nodded.

Bill looked him up and down and gave a strained smile. "Not bad. So you make furniture? You have to show me your portfolio," he said unconvincingly.

"You'll absolutely love his stuff. You two talk. I'll be right back," the fashionista said, and she drifted off to another pair of guests.

Bill said, "God, I love her. She's something, isn't she?"

"That she is." After a minute or two Maddox said, "Excuse me. I need a drink." He poured himself a double single malt and ate a couple of pieces of biscotti, which tasted pretty good, although nowhere near as good as Francie's brownies, and then he sampled some of the various mysterious-looking snacks. The room was full of botoxed strangers—media people and producers and lawyers and actors—with a couple of scowling artists thrown in for texture. He attempted to join in a few conversations but nobody seemed particularly interested in him. The fashionista was flitting from group to group, chirping and giggling in a droopy, manic way. The biscotti hadn't even taken the edge off, so he had some more. In desperation he tried to latch onto Bill, the designer, who was talking to a couple of gorgeous women. "Hey," Maddox said, and they flashed bored smiles at him. All three of them, Maddox noticed, had luscious lips—swollen Angelina Jolie lips, with a life of their own. He became conscious of his own mouth hanging open, gaping in fascination at Collagen Central.

"Oh hi," Bill said. "Sorry, I forgot your name."

"Maddox."

"Maddox, right. So anyway," he said, turning back to the women, "he's delicious, but kinda shy. I mean, he's from *Saskatchewan*. So I'm going to have to be Farm Boy Bill. Forget Rock 'n' Roll Bill, my fucked-up bellbottoms? Tight butt? Rock 'n' Roll Bill does not *exist* for this guy. But I can do it. It's all there in my closet. Farm Boy Bill is in my closet. Got the shirt, got the pants, got the hat." He put his hands on his hips and shimmied. "Girl, I can *do* this."

Maddox reflected that this was definitely one personality you didn't want to be living in. He drifted back to the biscotti and the mysterious-looking snacks, which tasted increasingly good. A woman standing nearby was giving him bemused sidelong glances and he realized he was eating compulsively. He suddenly felt very stoned, but it didn't make anything any easier. It was an intense whole-body kind of stoned, and he could barely move. All he could think about was how much he wanted to lie down, and maybe call Francie if it wasn't too late.

"Already?" the fashionista wailed when he told her he was leaving.

He mumbled something about needing to get back to Duane. "I think he's sick. He was shivering when I left," he lied. His jaw was so relaxed that he found it difficult to speak.

"Aw. The poor thing." The fashionista's face crumpled with concern. "Oh wait, before you go." She scooped the rest of the biscotti into a Ziploc and handed it to Maddox. "Here, take these," she said, folding her hand over his as he grasped the bag. She was gazing at him and for a moment Maddox thought of staying. He could lie down here for a while, on her bed, and wait to see how things would play out. She glanced at his damaged hand, then squinted up at him and cocked her head to the side. "Something I've been meaning to ask you," she said. "Just a quick question."

"Shoot."

"Ah—I was just wondering. With that electric shock—how did it feel?"

Maddox gave a quick laugh and shook his head. "In how many words?"

The fashionista released her grasp. "Sorry. Stupid question." She patted him gently on the back. "Go," she said. "Take care of poor Duane."

What I really miss about Francie:
5. She knows I'm feeling down when I play "Hey Joe" over and over.

It was late and he was too wasted when he got home last night, so Maddox never did get to speak to Francie, even though she'd left him two messages. Her voice sounded small and needy the second time, saying, "Me again. Just wanted to talk. Where are you?"

It's already Saturday evening and he still hasn't called back. He turns off the TV, picks off the stray bits of nachos that have landed on his T-shirt and pops them into his mouth, and reaches for the cordless phone. Duane stirs, looks up at him and sighs deeply. Maddox dials the number but nobody answers. Eventually he gets the commune's answering machine and hangs up without leaving a message.

He goes into the kitchen and opens the fridge. Not much in it except beer, milk, bread and salsa. Not much in the freezer either, other than the fashionista's Ziploc. He eats a couple of pieces of biscotti while he watches Duane come hobbling through the kitchen door. "This is ridiculous, you know that?" Maddox says. "We have to get you a prosthetic leg." Duane thumps his tail expectantly against the linoleum. "Sorry boy, there's fuck-all to eat here. Wanna go pick up a couple of burgers?"

He helps Duane onto the front passenger seat of the pickup and heads for the drive-thru. When their order is ready he pulls into a parking bay, unwraps Duane's burger (no mustard, no pickles) and lays it on the seat between them. The whole thing's gone in two seconds flat except for half the bun, and then Duane whines for more so Maddox tosses him a few fries. The dog inhales them and starts whining again, shuffling until he falls sideways against the backrest. "Forget it," Maddox says, turning away and looking out the side window while he eats. When he finishes he sits there and watches the traffic a while, then starts the engine, pulls up alongside a garbage receptacle, opens the window all the way and plays garbage-bin basketball with the balled-up wrappings and Duane's unfinished bun. "You ready to go home?" he says to Duane, but when he's about to make the turn he changes his mind and heads in the opposite direction.

The commune is a sprawling place on the northeastern outskirts of the city. A big tattooed guy who looks like an ex-con is standing and smoking outside. He eyes Maddox and Duane as they approach and Maddox wonders if this is Trucker Dan.

"Hi," Maddox says. He can hear people singing in the distance. "Francie here?"

The guy nods, takes a final deep drag and flicks the cigarette away. "I believe so." He smiles down at Duane, jerks his head to indicate that Maddox should follow him and they go around the side of the house, slowly because of Duane, to the backyard. The Born-Agains are sitting around the campfire on lawn chairs or cross-legged on the grass. They're all glowing in the firelight and singing religious songs. Someone's playing bad acoustic guitar and the others shake tambourines or clap or do a little hand jive on the beat. When they notice the ex-con/Trucker Dan standing there with Maddox and Duane, the singing falters and peters out. Francie, who has her back to Maddox, turns, gives a little squeal and claps her hand over her mouth as she scrambles to her feet.

"Is something wrong?" she whispers when she reaches him.

Maddox is trembling. He shakes his head and she hugs him. Her long hair is tousled and her face and neck are soft and hot from the fire. "I tried calling," he says.

Francie takes his hand and squeezes. "This is Maddox," she announces to everyone, beaming. "My husband." They're all gazing at him with a sweet kind of wonder, as if he were a being who came from another world. "And I guess you already met Pastor Jenkins," she says happily, motioning to the ex-con/Trucker Dan.

Pastor Jenkins nods and smiles. "Come and join us," he says, pointing to the campfire.

"And Duane," Francie says, bending forward to pat him.

"Ah, that's okay," Maddox tells Pastor Jenkins. "I came to talk to my wife."

Francie keeps squeezing his hand and grinning as she leads him into the house.

"Do you call each other Brother and Sister?"

He feels her stiffen and withdraw. "What?"

"You know, like Sister Francie? Brother Dan? Sister Hannah?"

"No. Why would we do that?"

"I don't know. Just wondering. Were you toasting marshmallows out there?"

She gives him a slow smile. "Yes, as a matter of fact."

Her room is small, with two sets of bunk beds facing one another. She sits on one of the lower bunks and pats the covers for him to sit beside her. "This one's mine," she says. "I fell off the top bunk my first night here. Now I get claustrophobic." She massages Duane's back and he nuzzles closer.

"I got your messages. You sounded terrible."

"Yeah? Sorry. I had a bad day. I'm okay. Some days I need to pray harder, that's all. I need to ask Jesus to come into my heart."

Maddox leans back against the wall. Above them is a calendar filled with coloured stars, taped to the underside of the top bunk. "What's with all the stars?"

She leans back beside him and rubs her index finger over a star. "Impure thoughts," she says. "Every time we have them we're supposed to stick a star on that day. Victory is a day with no stars."

"All your days have stars."

"I know."

He says, "What kind of impure thoughts?"

Francie shrugs and looks away. "I don't know. About you mostly, I guess." When she turns back he sees she's been crying a little. Duane nudges his snout against her leg because she's stopped stroking him. "He's a nice dog," she says, wiping her eyes and patting him again. "The thing is, I can't stop thinking about you. It's like I'm missing my front teeth or something."

"So come home."

"And then what?" After a while she says, "There's marriage counselling, you know. At the church."

"What, through prayer?" he says sharply. He looks up at the calendar stars. "God. I wish we'd never ordered that fucking pizza. We should've gone out for Chinese."

"No, don't say that."

"Why? Because everything's part of the Lord's plan? Bullshit, Francie."

Duane nudges her again, his tail wagging. "Poor fella." She plays with his ears for a few minutes then says, "Weird how you and Duane have this affliction, you know? Both on the left side."

"Affliction?" Maddox holds up his hand. "You think this is an *affliction?* Christ, I'm not an amputee."

"It was a message," she explains patiently.

"What? For you? To repent? How come you always thought this was about you? Not once did you ask how it felt to be nearly electrocuted, you know that? Not once. As far as you're concerned it's always been about you."

"You're wrong." She shakes her head sadly. "I always thought it was about *us.*"

"Anyway," Maddox says. He sighs. "It's getting late."

Francie just sits there looking like she's going to cry again. Maddox puts his arm around her and holds her close. After a couple of minutes he says, "You know where to find me."

"Me too," she says in a flat voice.

He hates leaving her like this, in this Spartan room with her stick-on stars and all the relentless praying and self-deprivation. He takes out his wallet, because he has no idea how else to change anything, and peels off four $20 bills. "Here. Take this."

Her face goes blank. "Oh no. I don't want your money."

"In case you need anything. Please."

She gestures around the room. "Honestly. There's nothing."

He keeps holding out the money even though he realizes it's stupid. "Come on, buy yourself something. I don't know, a necklace or something. Or give it to the church. I don't care."

She refuses to take it, but when she walks out the room ahead of him, Maddox slips the money under her pillow.

When he gets home there's a voice-mail message from the fashionista: "Maddox, hi, it's Laura. Just calling to see how Duane's doing and um, I'm really sorry you couldn't stay last night. Hope you're both okay. Talk to you soon."

He starts to dial her number, then hangs up. He has no idea what to say. He supposes he could try explaining to her what it was like when that electric jolt charged through him; how the current had hooked him and he'd felt every jerking nerve and muscle contract hard around it until he spun off into a white fog. But that would be all.

After a while he gets up and plugs the Stratocaster into the amplifier. He ignores the phone when it rings. As he plays he thinks of Francie and how she is lost to him, and then the Born-Agains come to mind—the way they were earlier, all of them gleaming, their faces lit and floating like planets around the campfire. The phone rings again several times and the red message light flashes steady as a strobe but Maddox just closes his eyes and keeps on playing, well into the night.

The Riddles of Aramaic

Elise Levine

Your life is in my hands, is what Em usually thinks—and a green surge, voltaic, jams her jock's tight gut. When she leans closer over the pale and weak, laid out inertly in test-tubes of hospital beds, a bug-zapper sound commands her cochlea. She knows no-one else can hear it. It is her privilege.

Stay with me, the loved ones shrill, rent with panic at the thought of being left behind—some make clawing motions at their throats.

They look like birds—hollow where they should be solid, entirely crushable. Others bellow at the soon-to-expire like pricked bulls.

Don't go.

Not Em. She apprises the curdled skin and damp kitten sighs, brows furrowed with suffering. Go, is what she thinks. Let me help you. I am blessed.

This morning, though, she feels irritable. A black mood jimmies her veins, equal parts guilt, shame, desire—the tumblers of a lock tidying into place.

The patient—a man only recently delivered by Team Oncology into an awareness of his metastasizing condition—blinks at the acoustic-tile ceiling like a newborn. Opposite Em his wife strokes his arm, calmly gazing at him as she sits in her chair with unfussy composure. Today she is a neat package: her fancy pants staunchly creased, pale-blue driving mocs the colour of her eyes. Hair expertly highlighted, warm copper graining rich mahogany.

Yesterday she'd undone. Head down, neck jutted forward, she'd charged up to Em's table in the cafeteria, despite only having met her the previous afternoon, and clearly oblivious of how Em'd had to push for this first date over sour coffee with the nose-and-throat specialist.

Tell me, the woman had honked. You're the expert. What am I supposed to say to our friends? Sorry, can't do dinner Saturday, Ken'll be dead by then?

Two months into her residency in clinical pastoral education Em has grown certain of one thing: grief makes people greedy, selfish as insects. She'd stared back at the hunched-over creature, whose name, Em had only then recalled, was Marta. Her face was bloated, almost engorged. Like a tick.

The doctor—knee-jiggling perfectionist handsome with high forehead and narrow wrists, high strung, twice-married—recoiled fastidiously, excused himself and fled.

Em felt a cold spray of annoyance at the top of her head, crystals glittering into the bucket of spite one at a time. She allowed a cruel micro-smile to laminate her lips, and settled in. Soon the gestures would trip across Marta's visage as they had for others, the visible spasms of the snakes and ladders of inner reckonings: self-recrimination, incendiary hopeless rage, despair—self-justification if the person was lucky or insensate or both. In anticipation Em actually pushed back her paper cup and danced her fingertips on the table-top: rat-a-tat-tat.

Instead Marta flicked straight, her expression blade bright—as if she'd discovered she herself could flay back the rind of the matter, get to the pith of the thing, it's heart: she would be a widow shortly, but for the moment that was inconsequent, because she knew her enemy now. She looked almost happy with the knowledge.

Em had run yesterday evening to shake the scene. Humility, mortification, forgiveness: counting streetlamps, cars, her breath between this curb and that (she is a counter, she'd count the bats slopping through the heliotrope twilight if she could be sure of each smudged shape), she'd done a sixteen-miler, 7:50 pace, her marathon tempo, cycling through to a serviceable redemption, flanked by night as she stretched. She hadn't behaved *that* badly had she?

Today she's really paying, pain, Ibuprofen galore. She cautiously stretches her legs in front of her while behind her the sheers covering the windows gasp silently in the hospital's air system. Her left achilles is hot. A cranky yawn stalks her throat, blooms like a weed in the back of her mouth. Her jaw pops suppressing it.

Behind her Em hears the squish of a nurse's shoes, the occasional brusque clog of a surgeon making the rounds, the routine checking of fresh incisions. Sequestered here in this private room, the footprints cause her to feel even younger than she is—in this world but not of it. Cribbed, while the crackerjack adults make haste, lay waste around her, busy with their ancient bustling pathways. She feels drained, absorbed against her will by a familiar, tedious longing to be swept up.

She's missed out on something. Personal suffering for instance—her own. Its absence is an itch she can't locate, crawling uselessly around her scalp. Studying hard, paying for a portion of her way through divinity school by temping part-time in the registrar's office, inwardly searching (wrestling with psyche-shredding doubts might be overstating the case) before becoming certain that her true vocation—her calling—is to facilitate the delicate transmissions between the dying and the living: all in the service of her effort to compensate.

But right now, with Ken and Marta, Em recognizes an intimacy from which she's excluded, a circuit from which she is barred. The effect is hypnotic, evokes in her a stale yearning. She has a mental picture of half-gnawed graham crackers scattered around the base of a milk-stained glass, detects emerging into the bottom of the frame two tiny child fists, her own, while an enclosing cyclorama revolves clockwise and she feels—she's not sure what. Returned or something. Unworthy. Verry verry sleepy.

She steals a glance at the wall clock above the door, then Marta. With a start Em realizes the woman has been watching her. Em looks away embarrassed but not before she notices Marta's eyes are soft and round as if rinsed clear. Such serenity, pure, unravageable. Obnoxious. Defiant even. A warning.

Brushing her teeth at night, Ken and Marta, Marta and Ken: Em worries them around in her head. Two weeks ago he'd looked in the mirror, shaving, and suddenly crumpled over as his spine gave way—bone against bone corrading to dust was the first sign of illness, what a shocker. He's going fast, whoosh, faster than medicine can prevent let alone predict. Em scrubs away at her mouth, pictures Einstein looking in the mirror and thinking of eternity. She blanks. Then another image comes to her, a man in racing shorts and singlet trying to outpace death, wings of ash lathering from his athletic shoes to indicate impotent speed. There: Ken does make Em feel spiritual. Visionary almost. He's like a crystal ball she can gaze into and see anything she wants.

Or could if it weren't for Marta. Brushing an invisible crumb from Ken's shoulder, smoothing his brow, caressing his earlobe—Thirsty? she keeps asking, he keeps smiling gratefully. Such marital bliss—putting aside yesterday's outburst it is as much in evidence and as implacable as a plain butter dish—is a wedge between Em and her meditations. She can't intuit imperfections, pulled threads, wrinkles, handholds for her journey into elevated realms from which she might contemplate humankind's dark wormy soul—harrowed, harried, embittered at finding itself not long for this world. Never long enough.

What else is she supposed to get out of this, what's it all to her without that vertiginous short-cut to god? (That non-denominational, non-anthropomorphic, non-culturally determined cynosure of holiness: Em is progressive, unfettered. Was profiled last year along with several other maverick pastors-in-training in a sleek, large urban centre magazine, which dubbed them The New Ecumenicals.)

She spits into the sink, tries imagining man and wife's couplings: him on top of her, a loving push in the bush—but tender, mutually respectful is as far as Em can penetrate. She's distracted by the sounds of her mother and father in the den next door, their TV on, the murmur of their voices rising and falling above the shush of running water. The clink of ice in their nightly glasses of diet ginger ale—her nice old parents, it's as if they're pickled in it.

She turns off the tap, leans forward and rests her elbows on the countertop, shields her head with her palms: hello inertia.

Greetings from the Northwoods!

So begin her e-mails to her friends, followed by a smiley face icon. The missives are becoming increasingly less frequent and sincere. When she'd applied to do her residency in this small city in which she'd grown up—it was the cheapest alternative by far, four months' rent-free living with ma 'n pa—she'd managed to look forward to early morning runs on dew-aquiver forest trails, sunsets blushing off the lake on her post-work rambles past her old nostalgia-soaked haunts. On her days off there'd be late-afternoon barbecues on the patio, platters of grilled corn she'd pick and shuck herself, the neighbours' seven-year-old twins tripping through the sprinkler on her parents' lawn, stubbed toes, crying, Em proffering comfort like frosty tumblers of pink lemonade.

It would be—she can't remember *what* she'd thought as she finished her term papers, plowed through her finals, aced her Greek and Latin exams.

In the bathroom she doffs her self-made skullcap, places her chin on her overlaced knuckles, meets her own image. Dusting of freckles over fine-pored alabaster skin. Clara-bow mouth. Lucid grey eyes. She is pretty and smart, in the fall she will solve the riddles of Aramaic (smile). Somehow she'd allowed herself to forget what it was like to endure the constrictions of this house, where you always knew who was in the room next door and the one next to that—a comfy cozy house with the kind of domestic overcrowding endemic to the middle-class, the middle-class that's almost extinct, a tableau vivant behind dusty glass that you might pass without a second glance in a museum (frown). So? She'd tough it out, go about her business, get through what she needed to get through.

I did not have a loving family, she mouths, trying to convince the mirror. I *have* suffered.

An untruth. She'd had an ordinary happy upbringing. Cupcakes and sparklers, the picture albums to prove it.

A wavering image alights her head. A tinfoil tiara, rainbow cuff of candles. The dining-room chock-a-block with children singing. More tinfoil: hidden treasure in the cake, to be gleefully forked into and discovered to mighty chortles and snorts—it was Em's ninth birthday party, and the day before her mother had taken a peck of nickels, dimes and quarters, washed them, painstakingly wrapped each coin in a pocket of aluminum and dropped them into the batter, stirring well to distribute them evenly since she was the type of woman who couldn't bear to see even one child go without. It was amazing that no-one's little Judy or Jeff had choked to death as they pigged through a second or third chocolatey slice. Hard to believe that Em's mother had thought it was a good idea.

Make a wish Em! And she'd huffed and she'd puffed and she'd blown the house down.

She'd just had her first revelation: that she would like to hate her foolish mother. Too bad mater's behaviour hadn't been less pardonable.

Ever since, if Em concentrates too intensely on what she wants a tiny glowing disc kaleidoscopes an inch away from her forehead, her temples throb. She has to lie down for hours, nauseated, in a darkened room.

She shrugs at her reflection, combs her hair, puts the toilet seat down and sits to don her lace-up ankle braces. The braces help keep the tendons along the bottom of her feet—inflamed through overuse—stretched during the night. The goal is to prevent the scar tissue that forms around the plantar fascia if she sleeps naturally—with her feet in a foreshortened position, toes pointed down—from shattering when she steps out of bed in the morning. She twists her mouth to the side and makes a sound: glass breaking. She makes another noise mimicking the noise she makes when the scar tissue unpieces.

Ay yi yi. Her body is a Rolodex of pain. Bone spurs. Her damaged illio-tibial band, unstable patellar meniscus. Last year, just when she was ramping up her mileage in preparation for the fall marathon, a disabling, near-demoralizing stress fracture in her hip. *Oy vay.* Pressure building the past six months in her sphincter, ebbing, like a lava lamp in her left side, a what-have-you blight. When she scratches herself she can't find the sweet spot, wakes with welts on her neck, legs, back—something about the way her nerves are bundled. Oddly, not like most people's.

She leaves the bathroom and hobbles to her bedroom. On her pillow a stuffed Eeyore, dishevelled and grumpy, one-eyed ever since she'd viciously poked him with a stick when she was six for no reason she would ever remember. Pennants above the neatly made bed: high school races, college track and field team. The cheerful coverlet, dresser drawers full of properly organized garments, saps her.

Why are you moping? her mother and father would ask her when she was ten, eleven, fourteen.

They'd look concerned: brows furrowed, mouths tugged down at the corners. What one would expect.

I'm not moping, she'd say. I'm *practising* moping.

They'd wander off, her kindly confused parents, more befuddled than ever by their precocious impenetrable daughter. Scratching their heads, shaking them from side to side. It sickened her to watch them. There was nothing they could do to surprise her. She could have killed them for that.

She hadn't been unhappy. But she finds it necessary to try the idea on for size. Ever since her summer-camp days, when murky heat and cicadas chanting combined with rapid-onset pubescence to create an intuition of ambitiously mystical thresholds, escalations, ascendancies, she has wanted to make something. Of herself, the world. It is her struggle. She is a project she can perfect. A prize she must win.

As for her feelings—whatever they might or might not be— let them fall as they may, like a game of pick-up sticks.

She closes the door behind her and climbs into bed, having determined that the fitted sheet is stretched tight and smooth— any fold or bump will banish sleep. She pulls the top sheet over herself, and the spread. She clamps her eyes shut, summons a prick of white embedded in a ball of darkness like a stone inside a snowball in reverse. She waits for the light to throb and grow larger.

She can begin. She gives thanks, she is—but suddenly she isn't whatever she is or would like to be. She isn't however or however not she is feeling.

Her parents are in the hallway. Both of them talking at the same time.

Who's the little man? Who's the mucky ducky sailor boy? Oh he gives nice kisses.

Em can hear the excited arthritic scratching of Skye's paws on the wooden floor. The thirteen-year-old border collie was likely the last of what had been the family's long string of prize-winning herders. The den's walls were papered with ribbons, the shelves weighted with trophies. Her mother's bad back meant she could no longer attend trials and Em's father claimed not to have the heart to attend without her.

Em could never make sense of her parents' devoted canine love or their sadness now that so many of the pooches had passed on—adored, much-beloved creatures bearing names like Promise, Beep, Darin'. Em had never warmed to them. To her they were all alike—interchangeable eye-stalkers, foreign, powerful. There was seemingly nothing they couldn't overcome, except for the fact that they were dogs.

She rolls onto her side, burrows her head into the pillow. She can remember coming home from school soaking wet one rainy lunch hour when she was ten or eleven to find her mother kneeling on the floor under the kitchen table, massaging Beep's gums to calm him—he was petrified of thunder. Em heated her own soup, took down a bowl from the cupboard. She turned off the stove. She picked up her spoon and ate from the saucepan, pausing occasionally to watch her mother knead small circles above the dog's teeth, under his nose—all the nerve endings were rooted there, she explained to Em, keeping her voice low and soothing. The idea was to relax him, coax him from his tranced quaking and panting, tail needling between his legs. Em stopped eating, traced a finger around the icy ivory rim of her unused soup bowl. She shivered, feverish. Rain shot the window over the sink. This, she thought. Now this. She felt she was finally embarking, her life an avenging raft, onrushing.

Now that she's in her twenties Em finds it consoling to picture her parents growing verry verry old, their skin crêpeing like elephants but their memories fissioned, unable to recognize each other—toothless, noisily gumming their Pablum suppers like words of love gone rotten. Em would visit them, not often but when she could, in the nursing home. They wouldn't know her anyway.

She imagines their confusion deepening, widening, swallowing them up. Their eyes growing round with alarm, eyebrows arching as they search through their vast stores of gibberish for the lost syllables of sense, as if sense were a home—the houses they'd each grown up in and left forever to start their own family—intact but rolling away, the wind huffing and puffing and blowing it across prairie and moraine, hill and dale, those long-dead dogs of theirs chasing it down, their small sturdy bodies flaring flat open like flying squirrels.

Em is certain that in the end all her parents would remember would be those dogs.

She turns again onto her back. Sleepily she lifts her cami-top. She is proud of her rippled stomach, well-displayed in warm-weather running garb of shorts and bra top. Her abs console her.

Like counting sheep: she fingers her ribcage, enumerates guy lines and under girders, everything in order. A tender hurt pooling left of the mole above her right nipple. Desolation and pride. Ever the spanners into the works: she can still hear her parents. They're in the hallway, cooing at simple Bart, or is it Skye? When it's not as if he could peel them a grape or get away with murder.

We don't need you.

It is two days after Em's last visit with the couple. She's not surprised at the reception she's getting from Marta. Em has been trained to recognize and manage confrontational, blaming behaviour. The woman's anger and hostility are right on time, righty-o. Necessary stages on the path to her acceptance of the great event about to befall her husband.

Even so Em flinches. A loose jiggling sensation spooks the top of her head. Trying to ignore it she studies the gerbera daisies—three orange, and one unearthly looking, chalky pink—gathered in a white and blue vase that graces the nightstand beside Ken's bed. All the colours, all colours, seem so intense, vibrating almost. Lying face down next to the vase is a card, and a sprig of cherry red ribbon, glowing. Some cherished friend's or relative's gift. Em re-crosses her legs, quiets her hands in her lap. Soon she will say the right thing. It is *her* gift. Her right alrighty. She is chosen. Her skull tightens.

It's just not working out.

Marta sounds as if she is addressing a servant, courteous yet firm—that tweaks Em. Moreover it dawns on her she has just been dismissed.

Please leave us.

The woman is an affront. What would be right—that she spontaneously manifest a hairy chin, a provoking squint. Right would be for her to instantly transform into a toad. Em's dismay leaking to her soles is overtaken by a rising throb of outrage in her temples.

Please leave us, she mimics—and lets her eyes graze across Ken's prone, suffering flesh. The man himself has already almost completely withdrawn, cocooned with his own final inner preparations. Em takes her time, restful. When she is done she lobs a glance back at Marta, sees the woman's face registers open incredulity. A hovering second or two passes then her expression closes: hatred most psycho. Em feels dizzy. Behind her now-shut lids colour pinwheels, silver ethers pullulate.

Ghoul, she hears Marta say thickly.

Em's migraine recedes. She can begin to feel her cheeks stinging. She unshutters her eyes again and regards Marta with a surprisingly keen feeling of satisfaction. You *hurt* me, she whines silently to herself. Satisfaction morphs to wild raw relief. Marta's done it. Em can hate her back and feel justified. It's like unwrapping a long-awaited, much longed-for present. Birthday girl.

She steps on a dead rat's nose, shrinks away. Notices the testicles, wishes she hadn't—what, been the kind of person who would notice the testicles? Why should she care?

Steeling herself, she gingerly nudges the rodent off to the side of the track and resumes her pace, a 6:15 mile. She's doing interval training at her old high school, only a five-minute drive from the local marina—makes sense, she tells herself, for the occasional wayward vermin to show.

On the way to the track she'd driven through quiet residential streets, lawns and rock gardens amply, artfully lanterned, sentinelled by statuesque oaks and maples. Cars presumably secreted away inside garages and carports since the start of the dinner hour—inside the houses lamps were on, TVs. Rolling by she had an echoey fretful sense that there was something contained within these walls that she was supposed to know but didn't.

She rests, sipping the energy drink she's brought with her in a squeeze bottle. Recalling those coiffed homes she has a distinct feeling of unreality—in a corner of her brain skirl endlessly receding planes, rotating views labelled one through pi barely captive in water-blotched blueprints. She must be dehydrated, her body's electrolyte imbalance and depleted glycogen stores playing tricks with her mind. She swigs heartily from her bottle, hopes she won't have another headache.

She does another mile, undertakes another, notices a knot-like sensation where her heel conjoins her leg—tendonitis. A marked decrease in flexibility, as if she's growing a hoof.

She feels badly in other ways. Her earlier exultation at having duked with Marta has faded. What if she lodges a formal complaint against Em? The last thing she needs is to be marked, go down tainted in her files as a narcissistic freak with affect-deficit issues. Making it unscathed through div school and getting one's own parish was difficult enough these days what with everyone and their auntie getting religion—something about the toddler millennium, the tight job market, the economy. There is a rill of abjection along the skin on her back, a lacey ruff, a spongy mushroom-like sensation, a lamella burn. She's tired so she speeds up, a little trick she learned from coach Doug down in the big city, where she trains during the school year.

After a lap she checks her watch on the fly—shit, shit. She's working harder only to go more slowly. She can tell as she continues that her form is off-kilter, strides uneven and inaccurate, shoulders jutting far forward in front of her hips like some weird animal concoction. A jackalope—with citrine eyes and an amethyst for a heart, unnaturally animate, its locomotion strained and awkward as it transports itself. It—she, she wryly muses, walking, hands on her hips, stopping—would stink something awful. An annihilating, dreadful funk that would protect her from extinction.

She doubles over from the waist, halved. She stretches, panting. Lets her tongue unravel from her mouth and hang loosely over her salty lips.

All summer, on her ten, fifteen, twenty mile runs, the dying have fringed her vision like lashes, wheat-coloured plumes of grass waving at the sides of roads. Wish-wish. God-speed. She can't believe she might have jeopardized her position, such deliciousness. Really she can't.

She stands on the shore of the great cold lake, a light wind shirring her hair as she cups the small weight in her hand. She has driven here straight from her workout. It is almost dark, should be but the sky is silvering with cloud, lit lingeringly with damp, rain likely lickety-split. She side-arms the small rock.

My man. Way to go.

In school they call it a release ritual, a little something to help the helper find so-called closure. The stone drops into the water and sinks instantly—this is the corpus. Her own personal belief is that the psyche remains with her, in her, consumed, a mossy stone turning, polishing her inner walkways—those narrow refined allées footprinted with her legion of dead soldiers who will live on, a part of what she has experienced. Closure indeed.

She takes off her shoes and socks and wades in. The water is so cold. Within seconds her feet, ankles, calves, knees are aflame, shod in giant furry mukluks of fire. Then they're numb, vanished.

The horizon too. The shoreline, its cicatrice of grain elevators, bridges. And further in the dream-like contagion of buildings. All is fog, levitation. A minefield of sand and gravel and eternal sleep.

Ken's not dead yet, she reminds herself. She feels crafty, sly.

Then she feels restored, renewed. She is blithe in her belief that things will work out for the best: Marta likely won't complain and if she does no big deal. Em can weather the resulting storm. She is that strong. Believing, back at her car, socks and shoes on the roof as she unlocks the drivers'-side door, that she stands alone.

Refutation: a tattered flutter, ragged movement in the corner of her eye. A better look yields the shape of a man sitting atop a picnic bench, hands in his pockets.

What is belief? Hope, with its sunny unblemished contours,

shadow-less valleys. She wishes for fishes: that instead of legs he has a single scaly appendage, that he's a merman, her own clever fantasy replete with gills. That he has a great smile. He'll mean her no harm.

She smiles at him: this is faith. He doesn't return the favour.

She snatches her footwear, crabs quickly into the car and secures the door. She drops her right shoulder and reaches beneath the seat, snags the hidden canister of pepper spray and hooks it onto her lap. She peers out the side window. Better safe than sorry.

The man swings his beanpole self erect and sways forward. His face is raised and he appears to sniff the mildew breeze. A dim haze veils his eyes. The forehead protrudes. The skin over his face is waxen and for a second as he closes in on the car it melts away from his lips, baring pitted black stumps. He is carrying something. Before she can start the engine and get the gear into drive his arm scythes and a rock, or a tin can, a marble, hits the windshield.

She is several blocks away—a heart beat, a wink—before she notices the shatter pattern, as if once-invisible joinings embedded within the pane of glass have been jarred loose. She sucks at the roof of her dry mouth. Pray? She'd hate to overreact.

Ken dies quietly, Marta's fingers interlaced with his—the nurses tell Em. As if she would care—when as far as she's concerned her parents have also ceased to exist, they're neutral wallpaper, elevator music. When she makes an effort to really take them in during these last few weeks of her residency, she sees flour and fat bound with water, like those giant tasteless cookies you can buy at any mall, nothing but caloric content. Nothing she'd really want or couldn't live without. It's as if Em has blinked and like that, her family, those she must administer to—with their ponderous, mopey complications—are gone. She can't imagine any of them anymore.

At last she drives away south to the big city, to her final year at school. Heartland, wasteland, she thinks as the hours string along. At first she is glad to leave it behind, can barely contain her speed to a sober fifteen-twenty over the limit. Her teeth are almost chattering. What she is passing through grows increasingly insubstantial. Thought-curds, white spoor, clump in her head.

She rolls down her window, filtering, sifting the air for once-familiar impressions: dirt, gasoline. Nothing registers. Anxious, she rolls the window back up. Paste-on towns, croplands puckered with life-forms—calcareous crops, livestock too numerous and varied to tally—dragonflies and locusts pressing themselves in mad blurts to her car windshield: nothing but flat planes, a husked place. And how might she attach herself? Her own voice in her head is whispery, faint.

She takes her eyes from the road, a truck honks at her—only with a juddering effort does she keep between the highway's painted lines. She feels she is travelling great distances, gaining inches. She stops for fuel at a large interchange, is surprised to realize she's been in the car for hours, finds she is so stiff she can hardly leave her vehicle to scuttle from pump to bathroom where she pees forcefully, brutishly, like a goat.

She gets back onto the expressway. With one hand she fingers two freshly arisen bumps, one on either side of her head. She prods and pokes, claws. Mauls actually. Breaks off to glance at her nails and sees blood.

She has been getting somewhere, she is pleased with her progress—having put some real miles on her feet in preparation for the mid-October marathon, which is two weeks away. Seven more days to go before she can kick back and taper her training to easy short runs, carbo-load till the cows come home.

Five-fifty AM. She meets up with her running group, nods hello all around, unzips her wind jacket. She silently gives thanks for being in school once again, for having acquitted her clinical practicum not much the worse for wear. Over by coach Doug she spies the guy she's most recently interested in, downing an energy gel. A peacock of a plastic surgeon, likes to run with his shirt off even though the first frost is nearly here—impossible not to notice his six-pack and *tell* her those aren't pec implants. Put a shirt on! she wants to scream at him. Date me! she wants to roar. She has always had a thing for attractive, eligible members of the Hippocratic profession. So when, after the three-mile warm-up loop, he cuts out from the pack and heads along a thin defile of under-utilized track, she pursues, losing him instantly in the pointillist pre-dawn. But she's no quitter.

Welts of light through the in-between-season trees of the park, this great lake a damp grey bandage. Tenebrous tree-tops pitch forking, striating fascia-like into the echelons of infinity: another shatter pattern, rip in the illusory fabric of wholeness. To which she pays no mind, distracted by a stitch in her sinistral side, vanished before she reaches the underpass, revenant by the time she attains the harbour.

She is tired so she speeds up.

Among the pealing sparrows, what she thinks of as the doxological crows crying out praise in their midnight robes (though it's morning)—virus vectors, disease amplifiers sparked with scientifically proven intelligence—and bursts of iridescent starlings true to their namesake, tiny stellar jewels bust across the heavens. The inhabitants of the waterfront soft-loft conversions awaken, don the armour of themselves, the great city marshals its inexhaustible resources (she tells herself) as she bruits the footpath beneath buttresses of hickory, sycamore, vast plantings in carefully laid out beds. Not for the first time does she marvel at the foresight, the tremendous vision of it all—until not ten feet in front of her a man who is not her doctor-man steps out of the hedges, round blunt object in hand. If only she could just power by.

A schematics of rock, water. A dormant humming, subvocalize of earth and ants and worm castings, bat guano's springy bower. Mufflers of pink-tinted cloud, the early, growing traffic a bee buzz through contracting pipes of sound—her canopic skull in figments she can't hold.

Me, she manages to think as her limbic regions stroke out for good. Em.

As she is, faceless among the hostas.

A Large Dark

Kim Aubrey

Three and a half months after his wife left him, André had signed up for an evening watercolour class held in a Sunday-school classroom at a suburban church. He'd been looking for a way to get out of the house one evening a week, to talk to someone other than his son, the nanny, the people at work, to meet a girl who'd praise his paintings and let him take her out to dinner.

One mild Thursday evening in November, a fluorescent ceiling fixture was flickering and Barry, the white-haired art teacher, had lumbered onto a stepstool to try to deactivate it, while André, 30 years younger and at least 30 pounds lighter, pulled a muscle craning his neck and offering unhelpful advice. When Barry finally gave up and let him try, André balanced on the stool, searching for the place where the narrow bulb was attached but bulb and fixture seemed to be all one, conjoined and wired to the ceiling. He tapped the bulb, leaned over too far and almost fell onto Barry.

"Don't hurt yourself," Barry said, stone-faced.

André took one last look and jumped down, massaging his neck. "Why do they make them like that?" he asked.

"To torment us." Barry grinned.

From the portraits on one wall, past ministers, their faces grey and bespectacled, peered out over the rows of collapsible tables and plastic chairs while the windows of the opposite wall absorbed the autumn dark, reflecting the lit figures of the students within.

André returned to his seat, feeling foolish and clumsy. He was sitting directly across from the flickering light, which promised to give him a headache. He removed his glasses and rubbed the grooves between nose and eyes, then placed the heavy black-framed lenses onto the table in front of him. He considered moving to a free spot across the room but Katya, who hadn't arrived yet, always sat beside him and he liked talking to her and watching her chestnut hair fall across her face as she leaned in closer to her painting. He was thankful she'd missed his attempt at fixing the light.

Even without his glasses, André could see the reflection of the teacher's paper in the mirror overhanging the table at the front of the room. Barry always tilted the mirror so his students, tired after working all day, could opt to watch him paint from their seats. Consulting his reference, a photo of a seascape, Barry began his demonstration by floating cobalt blue into an orange wash. André relaxed his eyes, tried to breathe deeply. Tonight he hoped to let go of his perfectionism and allow the paint to flow onto the paper, resisting his tendency to overwork the watercolours until they made thick pasty mud in the shapes of trees. That had been last week's production.

"Do a sketch first to get the composition," Barry was telling the class. "Play with the placement. Leave things out. Put them in. Multiply, subtract. It's like math."

"I used to be good at math," André joked. But no-one laughed or even turned to look at him.

The door opened and Katya appeared in a red jacket, bringing with her the mingled scents of her spicy perfume and the warm night. André thought how he needed a woman to make his life add up again.

"How much have I missed?" she whispered, unpacking her paints.

"Not much." He fiddled with his glasses. He could never think of the right words.

"I used to live by the sea," she sighed, looking at the reflection of Barry's painting. There was a hint of the Ukraine in her accent.

"My father's family came from Kiev," he said.

"Shh!" said Miriam, the grey-haired woman who sat in front of André.

Katya's eyes were black with flecks of white where the light struck them. "Do you speak Ukrainian?" she whispered.

"No," he said too loudly, causing Miriam and her neighbour to glare at him, but he only noticed Katya's gaze which flickered like the unfixable light then returned to the mirror and Barry's painting.

André put on his glasses and watched Barry write in the details with a long narrow brush, a form of calligraphy shaping fine finger-like branches and a flourish of leaves.

"A few more touches," Barry said. "And it's done."

"You said I didn't miss anything." Katya frowned.

"I didn't want to upset you," he said. But she had already grabbed her sketchbook and was dashing to the front of the room to join the students crowded around Barry's table.

André followed her, wanting to say something that would make her smile in gratitude or even admiration. He watched her stare at Barry's painting, scribble in her book, then resume her scrutiny.

Up close, the painting looked sketchy and insubstantial. When André took a few steps back it started to gain strength. Its power lay not in its strokes and colours but in the way they played off each other, the contrast of light and dark, the illusion they created of moodiness and movement. The rocks and branches in the foreground seemed to beckon to the glistening sailboat on the horizon where the deep indigo of the ocean faded into mauve.

"I don't know how you do it," he said to Barry.

"Practice," Barry said. "That's all it takes."

André didn't believe him. He suspected that there was some trick Barry was keeping to himself, that to make the magic work he would need to find the right brand and shades of paint, the right weight and grain of paper, the exact alchemical formula.

He looked at Barry's palette. "Is that a new red?" he asked suspiciously, leaning over the table to point to a deep crimson next to the yellows. Some of the other students moved in to peer at the colour.

"No," Barry said. "That's just alizarin."

"I thought so," said Miriam, who had left her seat to take a closer look. "You're always suspecting a colour conspiracy." She shook her head at André.

He shrugged. "It looked different tonight."

Barry scraped the edge of a razor blade across the paper to make flecks of white surf. "I'm going to stop there," he said.

"Beautiful," Katya said.

The students dispersed. André followed Katya back to her seat. He watched her tape paper to a board and squeeze paint onto her palette.

"Is this sable?" he asked, picking up one of her brushes and stroking its soft bristles across the knuckles of his other hand, imagining Katya's lush brown hair falling against his skin.

"Just start your painting." She pushed him away. "Get on with it. You're up to your old delaying tactics. You have to jump in, get your brush wet."

"So to speak." He smiled. "You won't let me get away with anything." The place on his shoulder where she'd touched him felt warm. His shirtsleeve, resting lightly on his skin, seemed to kiss the imprint of her hand. Maybe it would be a good night after all.

He looked at his copy of the photo Barry had given the class. It was a little different from the teacher's; the boat was larger, closer to the shore and there was an island. He made a small sketch to get the composition right. Then he started to lay down washes, losing himself in the act of painting for a while. He looked up when Barry walked by, nodding at him. That meant things were going okay, so far. He painted the oblong of a big rock but he started to do the shadow too soon and the paint ran. That flower of dark spreading across the rock tweaked his old impatience with himself. He felt the bad mood rise in his chest and rush through his blood. Now he wouldn't be able to finish and the night was goddam ruined. Liz was the one responsible for these moods. The goddam divorce couldn't come soon enough. Katya was painting happily beside him, her rock edged and shadowed in three bold, innocent strokes.

He tried to fix his painting, adding more rocks to conceal the blurry shadow, using a palette knife to scrape away some of the paint and create planes of light where the sun hit the foreground. But when he stepped back, he saw that the rocks were too big and too much alike and the white sailboat, which was supposed to be sailing bravely out of the harbour, seemed to be drawn hopelessly toward them.

"I've had enough," he said.

"Leaving early again?" Miriam asked.

André packed up his paints and brushes. "I'll finish it at home," he said although he knew he wouldn't. "My son's waiting for me."

Intent on her painting, Katya didn't say anything, didn't even look his way.

"I'm done," he said as he passed Barry at the front of the room.

One side of Barry's mouth turned up, more a grimace than a smile. "You should try and stay for the critique sometime. You might learn something."

André shrugged, adjusting the shoulder strap of his black portfolio. "I have to get home and see my son before bedtime."

Barry turned away. André stood there waiting for something—another word from his teacher, absolution, praise for being a good father, a wave goodbye from Katya, a nod from Miriam. But heads were lowered, intent on finishing touches, and Barry stood silent, immovable, arms crossed, ready for the students to bring him their paintings so he could place them one at a time on the easel for critique.

André hurried out the door to the parking-lot. He pulled his keys from his pocket and, trying to find the right one, dropped them onto the pavement. "Fuck!" He leaned his portfolio against the black Jeep and bent to retrieve the keys, feeling flushed with anger, hot in his leather jacket. The November night smelled fresh as spring but he couldn't enjoy it, didn't know when he'd last enjoyed anything. He'd yet to finish a painting and each week it seemed less and less likely that Katya would ever go out with him, that he'd even find the words to ask her.

At home, he dropped his portfolio onto the floor next to Braden's running shoes, removed his jacket and hung it in the closet.

"Daddy!" his son's voice squealed from upstairs. "I'm still awake."

"I'll be up in a minute," André called. He unlaced his work

shoes, slipped on leather moccasins and headed for the kitchen, his footsteps echoing through the big, empty house. He imagined Katya sitting at the kitchen table with a bowl of hot borscht, her lips crimson from the beets. Then he noticed the dirty dishes in the sink and his familiar anger flooded back. He'd planned on making hot chocolate for three—himself, Braden, and Bridget, the nanny. Now Bridget wouldn't get a mug. He filled the kettle and switched on the burner. She always let him down just when he'd started to hope she was on top of her job. She hadn't even wiped the counters. She'd probably say Braden hadn't left her alone for one minute, that she was hired as nanny not housekeeper. But he'd been very clear about her responsibilities when she'd first arrived. One good thing about Liz, she'd been fanatical about the house, couldn't go to bed at night if the kitchen wasn't clean, or out the door in the morning without vacuuming the wall-to-wall.

He filled the mugs with hot water, stirred in the mix. No, he wasn't in the mood for marshmallows tonight. Braden would be disappointed but he just couldn't reach into that high cupboard, undo the twist tie on the bag, smell that whiff of vanilla. Damn Liz! Even a marshmallow could remind him of her, how she used to bake for him during what she referred to as her Suzy Homemaker phase when she'd taken a year off from her job at the art gallery while they tried to get pregnant.

He'd loved coming home to a wife fragrant with baking, her cotton pullover dusted with flour, her tongue tasting sweet from cookie dough or cake batter. He remembered licking a tiny smudge of chocolate off her chin as he undressed her on the living-room rug. When they'd failed to conceive she'd claimed that his enthusiasm for getting her pregnant was making her feel ambivalent, afraid of becoming what he seemed so much to want her to be—nothing more or less than a mother and a wife.

"I don't feel like myself," she'd said. "I need to go back to work so I can remember why having a baby seemed like a good idea."

"Fine," he'd said. "But no more ten-hour days or skipping lunch. Your body is going to be nourishing our child."

When she'd finally gotten pregnant he'd tried to persuade her to quit work for good, to leave those modern monstrosities of paint and plaster behind and stay home with the baby but she'd taken only the standard maternity leave, during which he'd spent two weeks at home, sleeping in with her, cooking big breakfasts while she nursed Braden, the three of them napping on their queen-size bed through the quiet winter afternoons. If he woke before Braden he'd bury his face between Liz's heavy breasts, counting the seconds to discover how long he could hold his breath, then tasting each nipple to see which one was sweeter.

"The left one today." He'd held it between his fingers while he watched the milk spurt up in a thin bluish fountain.

"Don't be ridiculous," Liz had said, turning away from him. "Braden doesn't notice any difference. You always have to be judging everything."

Even with Liz's moodiness those two weeks stood out as the happiest of his life but when he'd returned to the law firm he'd been penalized for them, his biggest client handed over to one of the junior partners.

André walked upstairs, holding the hot mugs out in front of him, watching for toys on the steps.

Braden was in bed, reading his favourite book—*Green Eggs and Ham*. His fine brown hair had been cut short and straight across his forehead by André's barber. The soft down on his cheeks and nose glowed in the lamplight which cast his shadow, large and diffuse, onto the opposite wall.

"Daddy!" He put down his book. "Hot chocolate!"

André set Braden's mug onto the bedside table. "Where's Bridget?"

"In her room. She got a phone call."

Long distance, he assumed. Better not be collect. Bridget had dozens of long-winded friends and relatives in New Brunswick where she'd grown up and lived until just a few months ago.

"No marshmallows?" Braden asked, showing André his sad face, lower lip pushed out, hound dog eyes.

"Not tonight. How was school?"

"We made poppies for Remember Day, to remember the soldiers who died. Mrs. Skinner put my poppy on the wall."

"Good." André sipped his cocoa, thinking of his high-school art teacher, Mrs. Flynn, how she'd praised him, misled him into believing he could be an artist. And now with Barry's terse encouragement he was trying to paint again. Liz would laugh at him if she found out. She'd always sneered at watercolours, calling them old-lady paintings.

"What about Winslow Homer?" he'd asked her. "What about Sargent? Their watercolours are more artful than those blobs of paint on a canvas you love so much."

"They were both old ladies," she'd replied with that mocking smile of hers.

Would she call him an old lady too? Would she call Katya an old lady? Katya's paintings made Barry's eyes light up.

Braden said, "We're singing a song for Remember Day in the gym. Can you and Mommy come watch me?"

"Sorry, Bradie, I have to work."

"Can you ask Mommy?"

"I guess so." A brief spasm snaked through his chest, a mere twinge of what he'd feel if he phoned Liz. Even if he called her, she probably wouldn't show up. She'd be too busy with her new job in acquisitions, paying ridiculous sums of money for paintings that looked like nothing at all. There'd been a picture of one in the paper yesterday—a plain blue canvas with a snaking yellow line, the sight of which had caused his eyes to itch. Katya's paintings had an abstract quality but they always suggested something real.

He grabbed hold of Braden's hand, gently squeezing it. "I wish I could be there to hear your class sing."

"That's okay. Mommy will come."

"She may be busy." She didn't see enough of Braden but the little she did was too much for André. He begrudged her any part of the comforting burden of their son's love.

"Goodnight." He kissed Braden's forehead, and turned off the light.

With the dark came panic like a rush of water into his lungs. He had to breathe slowly and deeply to make it recede. Tomorrow he'd talk to Liz. Right now he wanted to fall into bed and forget. Then he heard the kettle hiss. Bridget was off the phone, making herself a hot drink. He'd tell her she had to smarten up if she wanted to stay. But when he entered the kitchen, she was washing the dishes. ·

"Do you want some tea?" she asked, her face flushed and smiling as if she'd been on the phone with a boyfriend.

"No thanks. Braden and I had hot chocolate."

Even the back of her neck was pink where it met her shoulders. He remembered kissing Liz in that exact spot while she stood at the sink, feeling her muscles move under his lips as she shivered then leaned back against him. Bridget was wearing a T-shirt and flannel pajama pants. He wanted to stand close behind her and lift the T-shirt off over her head. But she was nineteen, exactly half his age, and Braden's nanny. He felt nauseous with fatigue and confusion. If only he'd worked up the nerve to ask Katya out.

"Goodnight." He rubbed his neck and headed for the stairs.

André didn't mind the morning drive; he listened to the all-news channel and reviewed his schedule for the day. But his drive home that night killed him. As his Jeep crawled along the highway, his bones aching with fatigue, he kicked the day around in his head. There'd been a client's complaints, a hint from the senior partner that he wasn't clocking enough hours, a co-worker's snide remark about his choice of tie—"Wife pick that one out for you, Andy?" Had that been deliberate cruelty? Did the man realize that André no longer had a wife? "You hate it there," Liz would have told him if she were still home. "When are you going to start your own practice like you're always saying?" He'd put off phoning her all day. He'd have to call tonight. After dinner. He hoped Bridget had remembered to cook the fresh salmon he'd bought at the market.

When he opened the front door, Bridget was sprawled across the sofa, reading a novel, while Braden sat inches away from the blaring television. He wondered what Katya was doing right now, tried to picture her relaxing after work in soft, old jeans like the ones Liz used to wear, but he couldn't envision her surroundings and realized he knew nothing about her life outside of class.

"Turn that thing down!" he yelled.

Bridget reached for the remote.

"What have you done about dinner?" He removed his glasses and rubbed his eyes.

"It's fish sticks and French fries," Bridget said without looking at him. "Yours is in the oven. Braden and I have already
eaten."

"What happened to the salmon I brought home yesterday?"

"I'll make it tomorrow."

"It won't be fresh tomorrow. That fish cost me twenty bucks."

"D'you want me to cook it now?" She stood up, hands on
hips.

"You can do it in the microwave with teriyaki sauce. It'll take
five minutes."

"So why don't you make it yourself?"

"Why don't I do everything myself? Because I pay you to help
me do the things I don't have the time or energy for."

"Well, I want a raise." She was glaring at him, challenging
him like a teenage girl standing up to her father. With her clear
blue-grey eyes, pink and white skin and the freckles scattered
across her nose, she could have been Braden's sister. "If you want
me to do all this fancy cooking I want a raise."

"We'll talk about it later," he said, suddenly exhausted. "Just
cook the salmon and make a salad while I change."

Bridget stomped into the kitchen. André looked at his son
still watching television and realized how many times Braden
had had to do this very thing—enter that other reality in order
to tune out his parents' fighting. He wished he could crawl in
there with him. Often he too sought refuge in television or the
internet or one of the other distractions life offered with such
apparent generosity—work, drink, anger. Painting was different. He'd followed it like any other escape route away from himself, from the memory of Liz saying that all he was to her was a
big mistake, but every week it led him right back to that
cracked place inside.

When André came downstairs Bridget was fixing a salad.

"Since I'm making salad for you I might as well make some
for myself. I need to eat more healthy. You've got so much junk
food around here."

"You don't have to eat the junk food. The chips and cookies
are treats for Braden, not for you to stuff your face all day."

She slit her eyes at him.

"You should be more respectful. If I was this rude to my boss,

138

she'd fire me in a second."

"So why don't you fire me?" She tilted her head so her reddish blonde curls bounced a little. A hint of a smile crossed her face as if she guessed why, as if she wasn't really angry.

"If you don't smarten up...." He couldn't finish his sentence. He didn't want to fire Bridget; he wanted to kiss her.

"I do my job," she said. "Braden likes me. I take good care of him. I don't see why I have to uphold your bourgeois standards and fancy foods."

"Because that's what I pay you to do." His skin was tingling with something like happiness. "I pay you to uphold my bourgeois standards and take care of my bourgeois child." Arguing with Bridget felt fun and bracing like a game, not like fights with Liz, which had left him feeling damaged and desolate. "And I pay you to help me create a comfortable, nurturing environment for him so that his mother doesn't have a leg to stand on if she tries to get custody."

"Will she try?" Bridget looked down at the rings of red pepper she'd just sliced on the cutting board, her splendid anger dissolved into sympathy.

He shouldn't have mentioned Liz or even thought about her. "I don't know what she'll do. She doesn't seem to know what she wants."

"She hardly ever comes to see him." Bridget shrugged, dumping the pepper rings into the salad. "It looks like you're safe."

"It's not safety I want."

The next day, he came home to a clean house and a pot of home-made chili.

"Have you thought about that raise?" Bridget asked while the three sat eating.

"This is good." Braden smiled conspiratorially at Bridget.

"Thanks. It's my father's recipe."

"Okay," André said, "but you have to keep this up."

"Keep what up?" she asked, wide-eyed.

"You know what. The cleaning and cooking, the stuff you're paid to do."

"Whatever." She shook her curls. The kitchen light seemed

to shine right through her skin, making it as translucent as one of Barry's washes.

André watched the corners of her eyes and mouth turn up into a private, self-congratulatory smile, the kind of smile he'd sometimes caught on Liz's face in the middle of breakfast or when she came home late from work and kicked off her high heels. He'd never seen Katya smile like that; she grinned openly or not at all.

"Is Mommy coming to my assembly?" Braden asked.

"I'm going to call her tonight." The last time they'd spoken, he'd found himself yelling into the phone. She'd picked up Braden from school without telling André first.

"This yelling is the reason I didn't call you," she'd said. "I'd like to see Braden more often but I hate having to go through you all the time."

"You should have thought of that before you left."

"We can't continue like this."

"Braden and I are fine."

"Sure."

"You think we can't function without you, that we spend our time moping around the house, but you're wrong. We *are* fine. So why don't you just leave us alone!"

"You'll be getting a call from my lawyer," she'd warned. But so far, he hadn't heard.

Next Thursday Katya was early. She set her paints beside André's. "I didn't want to miss the demo."

"We're painting a still life."

She wrinkled her nose. "I prefer a good landscape."

"Still life's okay. Maybe I can get it right this time."

"It's not about right. When are you going to learn that?"

"It's all about getting it right," he said. "Sometimes the gods smile and most of the time they don't."

Miriam was sitting at the table in front of them. "You have it all wrong," she said, turning in her chair. "The gods can't smile unless you do."

André frowned, suspecting the women of mocking him.

"You don't smile much, do you?" Katya laughed.

He resolved to work up a smile for her.

Barry was composing the still life—a watermelon sliced in half, one half lying on its cut side like a dark green hill, the other sliced into wedges, revealing their red flesh and black seeds. He placed one wedge in front of the melon hill and one behind, then added a spray of purple leaves partially concealing the bulk of the fruit.

"Okay," he said. "I'm going to start with a sketch." He roughed in the melon pieces and the leaves with a soft pencil. "I like that composition. It makes a nice negative shape of the background. I'm going to have a small dark—the leaves and the dark stripes on the melon rind." He shaded them heavily. "A large mid-tone—the melons and the cast shadow. And a medium-sized light—the background and the reflections on the fruit. You might choose to make the background larger and have a medium-sized mid-tone, but this is the way I'm doing it."

André thought he'd do it that way too. He'd yet to see one of Barry's paintings go awry. He watched in the overhanging mirror while Barry put paint to paper and without any apparent thought or effort conjured bright images. Eager to begin he followed Barry's lead, letting his painting take shape under his brush, enjoying the curve of the melon rind and the vibrancy of its flesh where crimson blended into rose madder. He remembered to leave triangles and squares of white paper for the highlights. He forgot about himself, forgot about Katya sitting beside him, the other students bent over their paintings and Barry making his rounds, until the teacher stood behind him.

"Leave it there," Barry said. "You've got it. If you keep painting you're going to muddy it."

André set down his brush. "Do you think it's done?"

"It's very nice. Especially that melon wedge in the foreground. You've captured the different tones there very nicely. I like this soft pink background and the feathery quality of the leaves against the strong melon shapes. Everything works together to set off that red flesh."

"That's a good painting," Katya said.

"Beautiful," said Miriam.

André felt his chest swell as when strangers admired his son. "Finally, I got it."

"You got it once," Barry said. "That'll be enough to keep you going until the next time. Why don't you start another while you're on a roll? And try staying for critique tonight."

André prepared another piece of paper, taping the edges to the board. He sketched the composition on a drawing pad. This time he'd make a large dark—a close-up focusing on the big curve and dark stripes of the melon's skin. But when he picked up his brush the blank paper made him think about his marriage and his hand caused the brush to tremble.

One night a few weeks before she'd left, Liz had taken his face in her cool hands, looked into his eyes and said, "I have never felt loved by you."

He'd stared at her pale lashes, the whites of her eyes. "I tell you I love you all the time."

She'd drawn away her hands just as they were growing warm. "You're always either finding fault with the things that are important to me—the paintings I admire, the installations and artists at work—or putting me on a pedestal like I'm this domestic goddess that I'm just so tired of trying to be."

"That's not how it is!" he'd yelled. "You're the one always finding fault with me. You never say it outright but you think I'm a failure, that I don't have the guts to start my own practice. *You* don't love *me*!"

"That's not true," she'd said but he hadn't believed her and she'd proven him right. All that stuff about not feeling loved had just been an excuse.

Even now his chest felt heavy with the memory of that night, how she'd lied to him. He started to cough and wheeze, then fled to the adjacent kitchen for a drink. He was feeling a little better when Katya sauntered in to freshen her painting water.

"You look flushed," she said. "Maybe you're sick."

"It's hot in here." He stared at her blurred figure, searching for his glasses in his empty shirt pocket.

"I'm a nurse, you know." She peered into his eyes. "I see sick people all day. Are you sure you're not sick?"

"Maybe I am." He'd heard her tell Miriam that she was a nurse but he'd forgotten; nursing had seemed too prosaic an occupation for Katya. Now she was leaning so close to him that he was able to see her clearly without his glasses—her velvety hair, her skin reddish beneath high cheekbones, the smile lines on either side of her mouth. He kept still, enjoying her nearness and the shimmer of her scent, feeling his breath quicken.

"Maybe I have a serious illness which requires lots of nursing."

"No," she said, slowly sizing him up. "You look all right to me. I'm more worried about my melon. It doesn't look well at all."

"Oh." He rubbed his neck, still sore from last week's attempt to fix the light which had been dismantled so that tonight only the shell of the fixture remained. When Katya looked at him, did she see what Liz saw? What Bridget saw? Lately Bridget had been moping around the house. Last night he'd scolded her for serving half-cooked fish sticks and leaving the laundry in the drier to wrinkle. She'd burst into tears, weeping openly on the sofa, making him feel like a brute. "I'm sorry," he'd repeated half a dozen times, kneeling in front of her with a box of Kleenex. She'd laughed then, reaching out a hand as if to caress his face but only touching one finger to the tip of his nose.

He decided to try one more time with Katya. "Show me your painting," he said, following her back to her seat.

"Very nice." The swirling strokes of red and orange made the melons look wild but still recognizable, unlike the fruits and flowers Liz used to paint before they were married—her large canvases laden with a dark, impenetrable mess of colour.

"You just need some highlights and a cast shadow here."

"Of course. I forgot the shadow. Thanks." She turned her back on him and filled her brush with paint.

He contemplated the sketch he'd prepared. It was okay but there wasn't enough time for him to start a new watercolour. He walked around the room, looking at everyone else's instead. Returning to his seat, he saw his painting from a distance and his face grew hot. It was amateurish, simplistic. His colours weren't as clear as he'd thought and the purple splotch on the melon's flesh which had seemed a charming rendition of a bruise now looked like a mistake.

Beside his painting lay the blank paper. He'd thought it had reminded him of his marriage because that's how they'd started—with a fresh sheet on which they'd both proceeded to fling paint and make a mess. But maybe Liz was the white paper, not blank, but exposed to some constant source of light which cast a blinding reflection. He'd thought his marriage was perfect but maybe she'd been telling the truth about never feeling loved. Maybe disappointment was what had made her restless and bitter, disappointment in the meagreness of his love. So stingy he couldn't even give his own son a marshmallow or make the phone call Braden had trusted him to make, inviting Liz to hear him sing at school. Or summon the courage to turn off that light which made the things it shone on appear either brightly perfect or horrifyingly blank.

He sat hunched over his still life, staring at the backs of the other students' heads, until Katya said, "That's your break-through painting. You're getting the hang."

"No. I don't like it at all. The fruit's too dark."

"It's stormy. I know I complain about still life but it's really the same as landscape, only on a smaller scale. You've got another seascape there. That melon's a ship."

"Then how do you explain all that pink?"

"That's dawn." Katya grinned.

"Don't say it's darkest before the dawn," André groaned.

"You rescued mine. See how the shadows ground the fruit? They looked like they were floating before."

"Let's go out for coffee to celebrate." He blurted the words, then remembered how she'd rejected him in the kitchen.

"I'm meeting someone after." She flipped back the hair on one side of her face as if tossing André back into a pond.

"Me too." He gulped for the breath he'd missed while awaiting her answer. "I forgot I have a date with my son for hot chocolate." He hastily packed his brushes and paints before Barry could catch him for critique.

At home, a strange red car was blocking the driveway. Liz's new car. André's hands tightened around the steering wheel as he parked on the street.

Inside, the house was dark. He switched on a light, listened for Braden's voice. Nothing. He strode up the stairs, peered into Braden's room. The bed was empty. André felt his heart plummet as if the cracks in his chest had finally given way, sending everything crashing. Liz had taken his son. But why was her car still here? They must be somewhere in the house. Why hadn't he thought to seek out Bridget in the basement? He knew he'd find them there—Bridget and Liz—all chummy, chatting like women do, no secrets, their men revealed, exposed. He hated her, hated them both for worrying him. He sprinted downstairs but stalled halfway, hearing a muffled voice. Heart beating fast he found himself calling her name, a hopeful, soft "Liz" surfacing from his chest. But when he got to the bottom of the stairs, all he saw through the open door was Bridget on the phone.

"I'll call you back, Mum," she said, staring at André.

"Where are they?"

"She took him down the street to a friend's. They should be back any minute. I told her you'd be home soon."

"She could've taken him away," he said, his voice breaking. "You shouldn't even let her into the house!"

"She's his mother. How can I keep her out?"

He took off his glasses, wiped his sleeve across his forehead. "You shouldn't have answered the door."

"Now I'll know." She spoke softly, careful of him.

She sounded older, nearly maternal. It had been so long since Liz had spoken kindly to him. He wanted to crawl into Bridget's arms, into her unmade bed.

"It's okay," she said as he slid his arms around her and let his forehead rest against hers.

He felt like she was pardoning his mistakes, erasing his failures, easing his guilt.

"I'm leaving in a couple weeks." She pulled away, her face as pink as it had been a week ago when he'd thought she'd been on the phone with a boyfriend.

"Am I that hard to work for?" he asked.

"It's nothing to do with you. I miss home too much."

He leaned toward her again and she let him kiss her.

"Whatever you want to do is fine." He felt a space open in his chest. He wanted to do something large and generous for her, send her home tomorrow with three month's wages. The thought of such selflessness made his chest feel even freer and more open. But then he'd have to find someone to look after his son.

Liz and Braden would be back soon. He hadn't seen the two of them together in months as she'd always arranged her visits to coincide with André's absences.

"I have to go get Braden," he said.

As he climbed the stairs his limbs were loose and soft. His neck no longer hurt. He went outside and stood on the sidewalk, arms crossed in front of his chest, waiting for Liz, in case she was tempted to drive off with Braden in the red car. The weather was changing, a cold wind piecing itself together out of the silky November night. His eyes grew dry and sore from staring down the street, almost forgetting to blink until he saw two shadows, one large and one small, move through the dark. He watched intently as they passed under a street lamp but the light did nothing to make their pairing less strange or less natural.

Stitches in Air

David Helwig

Dear N,

It is New Year's Eve as I write, and the others are all gone. The end of a decade, the beginning of another with the tip of a new millennium just visible over the horizon of years. I am invited to a party at Sam Pruitt's house. Through his family he knows the rich and influential men and women of the district, who will be in attendance, and he and his wife flatter me by this invitation since I can perhaps further his career. Jenny F. is invited for the same reason. While the celebration goes on, I am sitting at what has become my desk, that Victorian mahogany library table with an inlaid and gold-embossed leather surface, which I claimed from the original reception area. I said that the broad expanse would be useful for spreading out and examining and cataloguing materials as they are added to the collection.

There is no window here, but if I were to climb the stairs, I could look from the landing into the darkness and see flurries of snow drifting over the lawn, which descends in a gentle slope to the riverbank where a green flat-bottomed rowboat is pulled up on the grass. Old George who plants and weeds the gardens and trims the lawn has been away a few weeks recovering from surgery, a hip replacement, and no-one has taken charge of the boat and carried it up to its winter shelter. This afternoon as I stared out I imagined entering the shed to find the oars, then heaving the boat across the frozen grass to the water, holding the gunwales in my two hands to climb in, rowing out into the grey river, the boat growing smaller and smaller until it is invisible.

In front of me lie three pieces of lace displayed on their storage backings, a piece of *punto in aria* sewn in Italy in the sixteenth century, a collar of bobbin lace, from Ghent a century later, and a table runner of Victorian machine lace. No purpose except to please my eyes with these three bits of delicate workmanship, which I have just extracted from the storage files—I wandered there seeking a clue, chose these pieces as if they might reveal what I needed to know. Each has a tag carefully tied to a corner of the lace, and on the tag the filing code. The code consists of a sequence of letters and numbers, and each sequence has four parts, indicating date of accession, source, type of specimen, and storage location. With this system it is possible to look up in the catalogue all the accessions for a single year or all the samples of *punto in aria* to be found in the collection, *etc., etc.* This information is currently being catalogued in digital form as well. I take some pride in the clarity and usefulness of the system. During my months of study-leave, I made notes on the procedures used at the V&A and the other museums I visited and refined them to our purposes.

Lacemakers began their apprenticeship as early as the age of five, or so I have heard, and with years of work, the eyes suffered, and the back. Vermeer's pretty lacemaker, arched so charmingly over her bobbins, will be a bent, blind old woman, useless, her fingers locked into half-clenched fists, hunched in a corner, turning herself toward the coals of the single chunk of peat on the brick hearth, searching for heat.

White lace, and yet the three samples are all of different shades, a curious silver quality to the *punto in aria*, a grey tone to the sample from Ghent, and the Victorian machine lace the tint of thick cream. The lacemaker arrives out of the blackness each winter morning, her face mantled with blood drawn to the skin by the chilled air, and she takes her place at one of the worktables. Her needle begins its quick clever movement. Somewhere a circle of nuns stitching, one reciting prayers as they work.

Ladies and Lace. The title of one of the many catalogues on our shelves here. For most generations lace was worn over layers of heavy clothing, but a famous Yves St. Laurent cocktail dress has a scooped back of black Chantilly lace, the openwork descending almost to reveal the nether cleavage. *Why do respectable women dress like whores?* One of your *belle-mère*'s questions. She stared hard at me with her queer dark eyes when she spoke. I took it as a question merely rhetorical. I was trained as an archivist, not an adept of sociology. And my clothing was, like hers, discreet. As my makeup. *Butter wouldn't melt in your mouth*, she would say, taunting me, and then she would tell me about her apartment in *vecchia Roma*, walls so ancient that in one corner there was a shard of inscription in classical Latin. Rather than tearing down the old buildings to make new ones, they shored up ruins and built among them, what the architects now call infilling, so that her three rooms were of all the ages, going back 2,000 years and more, a Roman wall, a mediaeval wall, a modern wall, mortared together to make her nest, her hideaway before your father discovered her and made her rich. That apartment, she liked to tell me, was the place where inspiration struck her, one evening as she looked down on the street below where the families moved about in the *passegiata*, that slow daily progression through the neighbourhood, and toward the end of her crooked alley, she saw an old woman sitting by the door of her shop, her knitting in her hands, and as centuries unravelled, the old woman remained, knitting the same stitches a thousand years before, all ages were one age, the age of the eternal goddess of the skilled fingers, and that vision told her what she must do, what she must create, and your father made this possible.

Butter wouldn't melt in your mouth: I was pretty little B., new to her job and eagerly at work, cool, precise. Little did she know. And what am I now? Experienced, capable, living for my profession, they say, almost priggish, rather inclined to solitude. Jenny F. and I pretend to friendship, though we are not exactly friends. There is too much unspoken between us, and true friendship is impossible on such terms. She is in touch with you, from time to time, reporting.

New Year's Eve: will I write to you until the clock's magic is accomplished? After tomorrow's day of recovery from the antic hours of festivity, the holiday season will be finished, and we will return to our habits. I spent Christmas Day with my father in his apartment in Toronto, listening to him tell his dreams. He recounted to me over our morning coffee a dream of a half-derelict building. Listening to him, the house I pictured was this one, this Victorian castle, once your family home. In some dream future it is derelict, and with all its additions, overgrown, an insoluble maze. My father had come on its wreckage. Sometimes, he said, it appeared that my mother was lost in the distant rooms. The dream presence of his children reminded him that he was worried about G. She's not a bad girl, he said.

Driving back on dark country roads, a little snow flickering in the beam of the headlights, my beloved white Toyota humming sweetly and reliably over the road, I pondered the chimeras of the night mind. I recalled my single visit to Dr. Mudge, the hour I spent on his couch. I hadn't imagined that they used couches any longer. They were brisk and practical now, I believed, staring across a desk, offering stern admonitions and selected pharmaceuticals. I lay on that old leather sofa, unable to see the man behind me whose voice solicited my secrets, enquiring about my lesbian experiences, though I continued to tell him there was no such thing. I was preoccupied by my helpless position supine on the couch, wondering whether I should lie with my ankles crossed, thus appearing resistant and tight-assed, or whether to uncross them and so indicate that I was loose and available. As I took my position on the cracked brown leather, I began to suspect you had told him he could do as he pleased with me, and I could hear his breathing there above me, behind my head, and I didn't know where he was looking, what he was thinking, if he was staring at me, as I lay there, available, helpless. Of course I never went back. I made the appointment with the thought that speaking to him would allow me to be silent with the others, but I learned instead perfect retention and security, practised them adroitly, no matter how pressing the temptation to blab.

I stare across the room at the fabric in the large glassed frame on the wall. It is a very fine coverlet, woven in Cape Breton in 1845 by a Gaelic-speaking woman, donated to us by her family. The front of the frame is hinged so that the object inside can readily be changed. Many of the nineteenth century weavers were men, so we collect only the specimens to which a woman's name is convincingly attached. All this to honour the intention of our founder, your *belle-mère*. She was a little ahead of her time in her obsession with the applied arts as found in women's work and able to create the collection before there was much competition for the materials she desired, though the samples of early lace from Europe must have been expensive. Your father was content to subsidize her collecting. The sixteenth century flounce that lies in front of me was one of her first purchases, bought in Rome from a textile collector who also did a little discreet dealing. She was afraid that it might be a forgery, but all the experts accepted it as authentic *punto in aria* of the period, a very small piece of course, a narrow flounce worked by a needle-woman 450 years ago, a girl in an orphanage, I've always believed, being taught a skill like one of Vivaldi's violinists at the Pietà. Orphan girls, trained to needlework and music.

Punto in aria means "stitches in air," a fabric that is defined by what is missing, a pattern fabricated around empty space. Styles change; we are fickle by nature, always demanding novelty, the new-fangled, the untried. In the next century, that great void was no longer indispensable in the designs, but even when the solid areas grew larger, more thickly stitched, the fabric was always a net with openwork, a circumscription of blankness. Openwork. Cutwork. I made the first cut myself. Since then a pattern of fabric and emptiness, a net to catch memories. *Punto in aria, gros point, point plat. Point de neige*: what I would see perhaps if I walked up the stairs and looked out, a lace of snow over the grass.

I returned from England, and you were gone. In the silence certain occasions. Pieces of clothing retained your smell. I would arrive at the door, and turn the key in the lock, hear the deadbolt shoot free of its seat deep in the door frame, and I would shiver as I entered the apartment, for I knew that you had been here once again, and before I took off my jacket, I would tiptoe down the hallway into the bedroom where the blind is always drawn down, to stand by the closet looking at the rank of blouses, the row of skirts, the jeans and trousers draped with archival care over wooden hangers, examining each one, putting out my hand, seeking your traces. Or I would turn to the chest of drawers, a handsome piece of furniture in the style of the Thirties, finely grained veneer, the piece designed with an oddly mannered mix of curves and adjacent straight lines, and when I opened the drawers I sensed you there, what your elegant fingers had touched. Once I had traced you, the spice of your presence, I would return to the door, shoot the dead bolt into its sheath, hang up my coat and prepare for my evening which now contained, as a room the bitter scent of smoke long after the fire is out, you. I would shed my clothes and dress in those which held souvenirs of your touch, your fragrance, and I would feel your fingers on my skin.

I did not grow up with fine antique lace. The lace I knew was my mother's lace curtains, which were, like everything about the way she kept our house, a little behind the fashion of the times. My friend Sara had bean-bag chairs in her house and walls of barn-board in the TV-room downstairs, pieces of old harness hung on them. Oh B., I wouldn't give it house room, my mother would say of such outlandish gestures. She was a little older than the parents of my friends; she and my father had met late, married late, had children late, and I was late-born, five years younger than G., so my mother belonged to an earlier generation than the mothers of my friends, who wore jeans and tie-dyed T-shirts that showed their nipples. My mother wore cotton blouses and tailored slacks. She shuddered at the sight of G. going off to high-school in tight jeans. I hadn't yet reached adolescence, and I allowed my mother to dress me as she wished. I felt a tenderness for her, almost as if I had foreseen the future and must love her while I could. My dark hair was long, and each day before I left the house for school, she would comb it and her clever fingers would plait it in two braids tied at the bottom with ribbons. When she was done with me I was, in appearance, an old-fashioned little girl, and I don't regret it, since it pleased my mother, and she had little enough time left to be pleased. As I prepared to go out the door, she would kiss me and tell me how beautiful I was.

The lace curtains: I found them wrapped around her, the daintiest of shrouds. She had been looking out the window of our small house, waiting for me to return from school perhaps, and suddenly she had felt some distress, faintness, vertigo, and she began to fall, her fingers gripping the curtains, pulling them down, and as she went to the floor, the fabric entangled her, and she died there, too young for death, but it came to her all the same, and I saw her lying there when I entered the house after my day at school, and at first I thought this was a silly trick she had played. She made jokes, hid and jumped out to startle me.

She was always inventing games for us to play. My mother was full of life. How was I to recognize her death? I was a good speller, and once in a spelling bee I had successfully recited the letters e-m-b-o-l-i-s-m, but it was only a word, not something that took place in my mother's brain. The first thing I did that day was to sit on the floor beside her and begin to tell her about school, about my teacher, as if the pretence of normal life would bring her round, but the story staggered, words failed. In the silence I reached out to touch her face. It was growing cool, inert. I knew I should phone someone, but I couldn't think who to call. My father worked at jobs all over the city and the surrounding district, framing new buildings, repairing old ones. I never knew where he was on any given day, though perhaps my mother did. G. would be hanging around the school, or on the bus coming home, or hidden away doing whatever it was that left on her face that pleased, sulky, haunted look. I thought of phoning our doctor, but I decided he would be busy in his office with his patients, and I wanted someone to come quickly, to bring my mother back to life, to save me. So I called the police. It took a long time for them to arrive, and when they came in the door, what they did was to ask questions and write things down in a small notebook. They wanted to know where my father was, then they wanted to send me to a neighbour's house, but I wasn't going to do that, leave my mother alone with these two men, who were so very stupid and unsuitable. The police eventually found my father, G. arrived home, and they both wept uncontrollably, and I, since tears are catching as a cold, wept too, though it was not till the funeral, when I saw they were putting her in the earth, that I truly knew my mother had abandoned me. Abandonment. Abandon.

Lace curtains: you, hidden behind them, hidden behind everything. I should abandon this scribble, go to the party, chatter pointlessly with Sam and his wife, drink too much and find some man to take me home. That would not happen, of course. Most men are, for all their reputation as sexual monsters, cowardly. It is when they are in groups, of soldiers, teams of athletes, gaggles of bikers, that they grow courageous and commit gang rapes, excited by watching each other. The primitive horde. Respectable men at parties are all attached to wives or lovers or their sad memories. It is a human weakness, remembering.

Jenny F. will be at the party, my friend, perhaps my enemy, my doublegoer. We came here at the same time, she taking up her position only a month after I had taken up mine, and we have succeeded in working in harness—is that the right image? Are we two Clydesdales plodding side by side, two oxen in a single wooden yoke? Neither of us will acknowledge the yoke, which is, all the same, locked on our necks. We are friends; we are not friends. Neither is in charge. We are both in charge. Who was responsible for this organizational blunder? Your *belle-mère*? Her committee, of which you were a member? I think it was she, and I think it was deliberate, a refusal to give her visionary project into anyone's hands. If no single person was responsible, her influence could still be paramount, and was until her death. She might, in her will, have clarified the matter, but she chose not to. If two males had been left with this blurred definition of authority, it would have become a battle, and one would have triumphed, but Jenny and I have tolerated the muddle, and it's possible that things go better this way, that women are more subtle in their assertion of territory. Jenny is a sturdy personage, whose tread is firm. The red hair—or is that strawberry blonde?—is always clean and shining, and in a moment of abstraction, she will take a handful in her fingers and draw it across her face toward her mouth, hold it to her lips as she thinks. You remember that gesture, no doubt, from a time when the two of you sat alone together, and you poured out your heart to her. No? I am convinced of her secret knowledge, and how else would she have come to it? The Christmas present: *Something for a cold winter night*, she wrote on the card, and that too might have been interpreted in more ways than one. She is one, she tells me, of a family of five sisters, all red-haired. There is something unnatural, fey, about that. Five evil spirits gathered around the sleeping hero.

We shared an office in those early days, and we watched each other, sipping morning coffee, afternoon tea, exchanging small confidences. We would go to our places at our separate desks, and I would think of you, as I feigned concentration on my work, my plans for the storage and cataloguing of the collection, the design of the downstairs spaces.

And this office, where I scribble these pages, after a long lingering out of days, after expectation and disappointment and strange fulfillment, would be all new to you. Or have you kept a key to the building? Do you come in the dark of night, knowing the code for the alarm?

I keep my diaries locked up. It is not just the desire to leave your touch on my garments that brings you in my absence, but the desire to know what I might have written about you, how many of your secrets I have told. I keep the words hidden. Memory catches a hint of an event, and then I bring out the hidden diary and find details that had been lost, how you stood by the door of the building waiting for me to put myself in order, gazing out, silent.

The Victorian lace, appliqué on machine net, has in its design a cornucopia, the horn of plenty, with its spill of flowers and fruits. Plenteousness, all the things that have happened, might have happened, came and went unobserved. Part of the superfluity of history, here collected, the excess, the overflow. Put away the pieces of lace, return them to their place in the cabinets of the fabric-room, temperature and humidity controlled, the air filtered to keep out moulds. Before touching them I put on gloves. I am always startled by seeing my hands in the white cotton, blank hands, awkward, unfeeling fingers. I think of undertakers handling the dead, though almost certainly they wear latex gloves. Since the cotton gloves must fit many sizes of hand, they are shapeless, generic, flattened things, like a child's crude outline of a hand, without the subtle differences in shape of the fingers, the varied length and placement of the phalanges, the slight bend perceptible past the last joint. The idiosyncrasies that G. would look for in my hands when she had decided to tell my fortune, on rainy evenings of the summer after our mother died. I would hold out my hand to her, afraid not to, and she would run her fingertips over the skin, searching out bends and hollows, and examining the lines of the palm, and then she would frighten me with her auguries, what was meant by the length of the fourth finger on my left hand, the shape of my thumb. In the white gloves, all these particularities are shrouded, indeterminate, and an awkwardness occurs in the grasp and articulation.

Years later when I went to visit a psychic in a bare room at the front of a house on Bathurst Street, she was less polished than G., less dramatic and thrilling, bored was the impression she gave, and her English wasn't very good, but once she began to speak there was a certain flat conviction to her words, as if she was reading from a text already prepared for her. She knew she had powers, but she took it for granted; it was as ordinary as the ability to do mental arithmetic. What she said was accurate about the past, my mother's death, and then she predicted you. *He come to you, this beautiful man, then he go. You happiness. You unhappiness. Always to keep secret.* A few more words then her crooked hand with its plump palm, some kind of stain in the cracked skin as if she had been soaked in tea, set down my hand and that was the end.

Careless, daring, I left these pages unguarded on the desk while I returned the lace to the cabinets. Anyone might have glanced through them. While I was in the pure filtered air of the vault (while you were reading my words), I opened another drawer, at random, and there lay a needlework picture that I had all but forgotten, a stitching of colours on a backing of coarse canvas, the kind of thing used for samplers—of which we have several exceptional examples. What I brought out with me is not a sampler—the work of a clever girl, with a name, Alice Morrow, and a date, 1879—but is in fact a stitched portrayal of a child, in a white dress, and behind her, a landscape, evergreen trees and flower gardens, and in a top corner a white house with a green roof, the mullioned windows little rectangles of black. The needlewoman attempted to give a sense of dimension by lighter and darker shadings, but still the face of the child is flat and naive, a round face with red lips, wide eyes and dark hair, bland as milk, sweet as honey. Perhaps that was what my mother wished for me as well. She made me a dress of fine white cotton, gathers and stitches of smocking on the front, and I would wear it as we visited my great-aunt Lil, who would offer me a humbug from the dish at her chair. I tried to keep still and not cause my mother distress by my twitching and poking where the stiff fabric of the dress itched my skin. I knew, as a child, that my mother was in danger, that she was a treasure on loan which might be called back at any time. And was. They put makeup on her, the undertakers, my mother who had never in her life worn makeup, whose scrubbed skin and brushed hair were testimony to a scrubbed and brushed character, and when G. saw her there, lipsticked, rouged, she made a scene—they had turned her mother into some kind of doll. G., always the bad daughter—who refused to visit aunt Lil, wore her sweaters too tight, her skirts too short, to our mother's dismay—now out of her bad, crazed love would have seized the body in the satin-lined box and thrown it on the floor and scrubbed the face until it looked like our mother, had she not been dragged away. Myself, I was abashed and proper, or pretended to be so. It was a role I had mastered.

Makeup: I liked you to watch me as I rubbed foundation into my skin, lightly shaded my cheeks with a brush, a smaller brush to spread lipstick on my mouth, one finger drawn over my eyelid with a hint of eyeshadow. My dark, long eyelashes have no need of mascara, but once, tempted by something you had said, I coated them grotesquely, thickened the eyeshadow, painted my mouth large with a dark gloss, posing so you could stare at my false face.

The needlework girl turns her expressionless eyes away from the sight of us, and she walks the lines of cross-stitching back to the garden, where the red tulips, embroidered in silk thread, catch her glance, and then she shrinks into the perspective distance, where everything is minuscule and neat, past a little patch of forget-me-nots, each no more than one tiny blue stitch, and she enters the inch-high house where life waits for her, duties, the cold rooms to be cleaned with broom and cloth, her husband to be attended in his sickness, the rigours of childbirth. She is the perfect wife.

You seldom spoke of your mother, though it was what our histories had in common, the loss of a parent. The person who spoke of her was your *belle-mère*, who had composed a list of her perfections, which she would recite in your presence, you severe, perhaps displeased, but never speaking your displeasure. It was one of her ways of attempting to take possession of you, that recitation, claiming you for her own. If she invented your mother, your mother's son came into her keeping. I averted my gaze from the dark eyes, set close together with an oddity of placement of the iris, a hint of strabismus, so that her dark gaze was fixed and narrow. It added to the force of her looks, as I sat across the table from her in the early meetings of the committee, battling to assert my independence, my professional competence, though I was her creature. Later she wished to send me to England, and I went. When I returned to find you gone, she was different, as if moved by other interests now. We were, both of us, broken by your loss. Or perhaps she saw only that I was no longer capable of defiance. She did not need to exhibit her mastery of me. She had wished to prove herself to you, but of course everyone did. I would notice how in your presence Jenny F. chose her words with especial care, held herself very upright. Proud flesh. Yet you were soft-spoken, undemanding, though with that edge of coldness, as if something in you could never be touched, the structure of bone. Osteology. He is an untouchable man, Jenny F. said to me the day she arrived. I was put on my mettle by that remark. And if I were to go to that New Year's party, to stare into her green cat's eyes? All of the five sisters have green cat's eyes.

I heard a voice in the hall upstairs, went to look. Nothing. The lights out except those that remain on all night as a deterrent to burglars and vandals. By the front door, the desk where Yvonne sits, our new receptionist—a tall breastless, hipless girl with a long, strangely beautiful face, a slight bump at the bridge of the nose, a high brow with straight hair drawn back from it, a face from an old Flemish painting. Her husband is one of those weedy boys with an unthriving bit of whisker at the end of his chin. I wonder how they are passing this New Year's Eve. Perhaps quietly toking up with a few equally thin and silent friends. In university I spent weekends like that, smoking up and eating subs. Waiting. At work Yvonne sits at her desk with our reprint of *Le Ménagier de Paris*, the words of an ageing man as he writes out advice for his young wife, moral disquisitions, recipes. Yvonne says she plans to make it into a novel. Behind her desk are postcards of mediaeval manuscript illuminations, scenes from ordinary life, three women baking bread in an outdoor oven. Perhaps she's thinking about her novel as she sits with her friends, a little high, listening to a Cowboy Junkies tape. Outside the windows, the earth is veiled in *point de neige*. In the darkness I can make out the hull of the rowboat, the gunwales traced in white lines, two curves that meet at the bow as the two flat seats collect the falling flakes. That voice again: I have already looked, and found no-one, though the old house is a kind of maze that might hide an intruder, the narrow halls and back staircases and doors that lead to other doors. Everything prompts suspicions. You would know your way around the old rooms by touch, since you lived here as a boy. Here you lay sick with measles in one of the upstairs rooms, feverish, and in your dreams, terrible women hovered, avid as succubi, and even your kindly mother watching over you grew winged and vengeful. This was your delirium, and you walked in your sleep, to be found crouched in the attic defending a small animal that only you could see. You told me that so I would know that you recognized the succubus. Walls have been removed since your childhood, doorways opened, and in the basement the storage-rooms and annexes added. I never considered until now that the old green rowboat must have been yours, when you were a boy, your hands on the oars, hours spent on the water in silent contemplation. I tried to know everything about you, spying on you when you were away from me, and yet I missed the obvious. You avoided my questions, knowing I wished to eat your heart. One night I watched the door of your apartment from darkness until dawn, but even as I watched I suspected I was on the wrong track. A ladder at the back window, and you climbed down and met her in the woods by the shore. At dawn I drove home, phoned you, pretending to have just wakened, asking you to meet me in the evening, then took a shower, hot, then cold, and made my way here to work.

I watched you with Jenny F., knowing what I knew. Now you write her letters, a spiritual intimacy. The gift she left me, here on this table, was a message. The way it was wrapped, white tissue drawn into careful pleats with a bright red ribbon, like a fine cotton dress stained with blood. When I tore open the gift wrapping, I was at first puzzled. It was only gradually I understood.

In her sturdy solidity Jenny F. reminds me of one of my high-school teachers, though Miss Tate was not a redhead, but ash-blonde, her hair cut short, robust, short-legged, heavy-thighed, with plump breasts that she tried to conceal in loose sweaters and shirts. If I had wished to answer Dr. M.'s impertinent questions about lesbianism I might have told him about Miss Tate. We all knew, somehow, that she loved girls, though she was perfectly discreet in her behaviour. A gifted teacher, she made the history she exposited lively and personal. Yes, a good teacher, and she thought me clever. I knew she had a little secret passion for me. She made classes a pleasure, and I went to her at the end of the year to tell her so. This was my final term, and apart from a graduation ceremony, would be the last day I walked through the halls of that school. She was alone in her classroom when I came, and I was pert and full of smiles as I thanked her. She was, as always, serious, her voice measured and grave. I stood near her desk at the front of the room, and she was leaning back, her hips against the edge of the wood. When I asked if I should kiss her goodbye, she said nothing, so I bent forward, and as I put my lips to hers, I thought I felt her trembling, and cheeky as can be, I slipped my tongue into her mouth for a second, then drew away, met the pale staring eyes and turned from her, strutted away with a little switch of the hips. Miss Tate was not at the graduation ceremony. I was unduly pleased with myself over that kiss, so very daring and clever. It was only years later, when, to my surprise, she turned up here with a class of high-school girls for the regular school tour, looking older, smiling at me but saying nothing, that I thought I had been cruel. A lesbian experience for Dr. Mudge. Of course he would have had no real interest in that little story. He wished for something gross and sweaty. I might have told him how at seventeen one summer afternoon I allowed Peter Loomis to penetrate me, once I was assured that he was well-armoured in rubber. When we were done, I was embarrassed by what had occurred, how my body had gone its own way, sudden startling events, uncontrollable as blushing or hiccups. I hoped that Peter hadn't noticed. To distract him, I demanded he pay me $20 for the privilege of entry. He stared, wordless, unable to take it in. But you're not one of those, he said. Wasn't it worth $20? I said. I was relieved by the unsettling effect of my demand, his discomfiture, confusion. Things were back under control. I was aware that my rebellious body wanted to have him inside me again, but I only smiled and put out my hand for the money. At last he gave me two $10 bills, and I tucked them into the pocket of my jeans. As I was leaving the house, I passed his mother upstairs in the kitchen baking a cake and watching a portable TV. Do you have to go? she said. You could stay for dinner. No, I said, my father's expecting me.

A week later Peter was waiting outside the store when I finished work. He told me he had another $20, but I told him the price had gone up, and when he insisted on knowing how much, I said a million dollars and walked away. I despised him a little for giving me the money when I asked for it.

The stitchery-girl smirks at the thought. She is above it all, the white child who will be the perfect wife. Doesn't the perfect wife grow cold as the years pass, bored with the bedtime routine, preoccupied with your career and sociability? The perfect wife has difficulty distinguishing between her father and her husband. Men are much the same in a perfect world. The perfect world where I'm certain you must remember me from time to time, imperative, cunning, addicted. Like the villainess at the centre of your book.

The man behind the pseudonym. The lack of an author photo, the one-line biography are hints of concealment, but for all my pride in my intuition, I didn't catch on. I found the gift, red on white, blood on the snow, here in my office, and I carried it home in my leather briefcase. When I reached my apartment, I left it on the kitchen table, and it was only when I was ready for bed that I picked it up, tore off the ribbon, and ripped away the pleated tissue. I read the title.

Gray's Anatomy. I put the book down on the table, beside the white tissue and red ribbon and stared at it. With this strange gift, I thought, Jenny had introduced irony, always a dangerous step, for irony is a powerful solvent, and once it is evoked, the safety of a bland conformity is gone forever. *Gray's Anatomy.* A joke I couldn't comprehend. I reached out one finger and idly opened the book, glanced at a few lines, let it fall closed again, stared at the cover. *Gray's Anatomy.* Giggled aloud at my obtuseness. The book was a novel, using the title of the world's best known medical text. I laughed again, at how I had been misled. I opened the book, read the opening lines of the first page. *Long-*

boned, yes, the girl in his bed was long-boned and beautiful and naked, but unfortunately she appeared to be very dead. The first chapter of the book had a title. *Osteology.* Beneath it the lines I had read. *Long-boned, yes.* I flipped pages and found that each section had a similar title. *The Articulations. The Nervous System. Male Generative Organs.*

After the trip back from my father's on Christmas night, the last part of it in thick blowing snow that made the driving difficult and exhausting, I fell into bed, but in the night I woke from a dream about you. I was among trees, watching for you, and then I crept up to a cabin and looked in the window, and inside you were sitting at a table, concentrating, a pencil in your hand. There were birds flying around the room, but you appeared not to see them. I woke out of the dream. *N. is the one who wrote that book*, I said, speaking aloud. I turned on the light, took the book in my hand, and now, as I turned the pages, it all came clear. I remembered a friend in graduate school who had written and published a couple of short stories; they were, he told me, very closely based on real people, but the models never recognized themselves. You killed me at the book's end. Or was it me you killed? Maybe it was your perfect wife. The lady or the tiger?

You instructed Jenny F. to give me the book. And do you expect me to respond? Are we to begin once more? You are to be found, I know, if I made a concentrated effort. Now Jenny F. has put your text on the themes of our story into my hands. You have the last word. As you follow out the necessities of your intrigue, there are little reflections of an old reality. *They might have met in any number of ways, but they would certainly meet.* You and I were destined to collide, somewhere in time and space. It was inevitable, as the falling object is certain to strike the earth.

The first and fatal interview. Your *belle-mère* met me at the bus terminal—I was to call her by her first name, she said, but I never could—and drove me here, pointed out the bathroom where I might—yes, she said it—freshen up, and the boardroom I was to enter when I was freshened. So I emptied my bladder, washed my hands, checked my makeup and went through the doorway I had been shown. Three people sat at the long table, and one of them was you. *That is the most beautiful thing I have ever seen*, a voice said. A voice new to me, although my own. How does it happen to us, that we look at another being and are seized, changed, imprisoned, and in the same instant set free. *Who ever loved that loved not at first sight?* I had read those words, not taken them seriously. I understood impulses, preferences, judgments. Not this. Beauty is one word for the terrible recognition, the meltdown of the personality. I was nothing but my desire for you. I was brave enough to meet your gaze, those gentle astonishing eyes. I was introduced to you and to an elderly woman, a retired professor of classics who was chief among advisors. You were a doctor, they said, and I wished you to survey, palpate, cut me open, cure me. Then I was interviewed. You asked few questions, and those you asked were framed to make it all easier, lobs so that I could snap the ball quickly back over the net. Yes, you were being kind, as if you knew that I was wounded, helpless, in terror that I might be sent back to Toronto and never see you again.

Behind your shoulder was a window, and in the open space beside the river, a boy was running, trying to get a kite in the air. If the kite flew I would get the job, I decided, and while trying to pay attention to what I was saying I watched him, and at last the delicate paper ship lifted off. I answered the next question with more confidence. If I lacked training in museology, I could be sent for further study. The kite was high in the air, I would be hired for this job, and I would have you, even if, as was inevitable, you were married. No. Married to your career, to your high standards of behaviour, to some careful future, the perfect wife.

The meeting of the man and the woman in your book: that long description of the cottage at the edge of the sea, mountains behind it, the little beach among the tall firs, and your hero escaping there from the complications of his life, dead bodies, threats, conspiracies, and he swims in the clear water, the sunlit sky above, and then as he comes to shore, he sees her drawing, the pad on her knees as she sits on a rock.

She is unflustered by the naked man.

Does the perfect wife know that you have published this under an invented name? Perhaps she takes all the characters to be aspects of her varied perfection. Told her name, I have chosen

163

to forget it.

My return from England: it is always in the present tense the moment when the queer dark eyes stare at me and instruct me that you are gone, that you have married and moved to a new place. She will be the perfect wife, the voice says, and I stand frozen, determined to reveal nothing. She accepts my smiles and congratulations, while I hold myself upright, in defiance of the depletion in my brain that tells me I am about to faint. I walk away, lock myself in the washroom cubicle and wait for death. From that moment on, everything around me seems to be a little out of synchronization, like a dubbed movie where the lips and the words did not resemble each other. I live a life in translation.

That voice upstairs. Again, when I went to look, no-one, the halls dim as I walked through them, a light here and there to repel invaders. Standing in front of Jenny F.'s office, I thought I heard a sound inside, turned the handle and slowly opened the door, half expecting to find her there, and you with her, but the room was empty, beyond the window the manic dance of the falling snow. I switched on the light. On the wall above her desk, the print of Vermeer's Lacemaker, and two wildflower prints, reproductions from the Catherine Parr Traill-Agnes Fitzgibbon volume. We are close to the country where the Strickland sisters endured the pioneering struggle, bearing the consequences of their husbands' worldly incompetence. On the other walls are copies of Mary Cassatt prints, a print of a painting by Gabrielle Münter. Back in the hallway I listened, heard nothing but the various sounds of electricity, the buzz of a light fixture, the hum of the heating system. I recalled the night at the V&A when I had stayed working late, and on the way out of the building, got lost, blundered into a storeroom full of plaster casts. The huge copy of Michelangelo's David rose above me, the Perfect Naked Man, the figure so large it had required a fig-leaf fifteen inches long to shield his parts from the widowed queen's gaze. In the darkness of the storeroom, the offending genitals were shrouded in darkness. I could make out only the ghostly shape of the hips in *contrapposto*, the tall torso rising toward the ceiling. Ahead a virgin and child blocked my way. Beneath an archway supported by heavy columns, I stopped, hoping to work out how I had come into the room, where the door must be. Turned, and I was walking beside a row of empty display cases, heavy wood frames with glass tops, my fingers just touching them now and then. A crouching figure. A head detached from its neck. Arms. Legs. And I could hear voices around me, one voice at first, yours, but no matter how I listened I couldn't make out the words. The tone was severe, then coaxing, then once again severe. A second voice, a kind of duet with the first, and I knew it was my own voice. I had fled the prison of my body to meet up with you in this muddled obscurity. In the gloom I was hemmed in by severed body parts. It was like coming upon the wreckage of a great apocalyptic battle, stumbling on it in the dead of night, when the killing was over, the souls departed. I could not find my way, until at last I heard a door open, and I called out, and the security guard—a man I had often met at the night entry—found me and guided my steps with his flashlight.

Tonight no-one will discover me in this empty building. In the attic, where Sam Pruitt has his little conservation lab, the spirit of the delirious child defends the helpless furred creature. I stood by the window on the landing, and the thick flakes whirled and turned in the dim reflection that came from somewhere to illuminate their flight. Stitches in air, the boat vanished in the blowing snow, the current of the river unseen, unceasing. Out there in the winter darkness, eyes seeking my eyes, lost thoughts attentive to my need, the unremembered struggling to return. As I write this down, I observe the little scar on one finger of my left hand, the healing not quite perfect, in spite of your careful needlework. Stitches in flesh. Cutwork. Stitches in air.

Your doctor-detective will return in later books, and each will have the title of some well-known medical text. You will become pseudonymously famous, but the perfect wife will never know who is the author of these outrageous fantasies. You will encode all your secret moments in another thriller called *The Circulation of the Blood*, or *Common Diseases of the Eye*, eventually one called *The Interpretation of Dreams*. Dr. Freud is out of fashion, but it would make for an excellent title. You are onto a good thing—that delicious chapter called "The Digestive

System," in which the sly, obviously criminal chef explains to Gavin Gray the function of each of the knives on his carefully organized rack, this followed by the dinner with the young woman who chatters gaily about cannibalism. Yes, I wished to eat your heart.

That was one of the drawings on the wall, my devouring of your heart. Those sketches which began to inscribe themselves when I came back home after the momentous events in your examining-room, wild with triumph, unable to contain myself. I ran up the stairs from the street, closed the door behind me, noises coming from my throat, less than music, or more. On the table by my bed was a black felt marker I'd used to label a parcel, a birthday present for G., and suddenly I had it in my hand, and I was drawing on the wall, and writing, creating a kind of cartoon history of my triumph, the lips of your kissable mouth and a balloon with words, your inner thoughts, and I put myself there, the story I'd invented, oval face, dark eyes and tiny nose, poor little thing, helpless, frightened, and then my vast hungry mouth about to eat your heart. I inscribed a rectangle, and inside the rectangle I told it all, though words wouldn't contain what needed to be said. Once, when I was a student, I enrolled in a one-semester course on the history of love poetry, taught by a short, dry, acerbic man, who had no business, one would say, with such things. We began with the Song of Solomon. *His banner over me was love.* I drew a mountain and two figures, hand in hand, walking up the slope toward the sun.

I was unable to tell where your body ended and my own began. It was you who stood in my bedroom drawing in heavy black lines on the pale green wall. I laughed. It was ridiculous and wonderful. I would sit in my white wicker rocking chair and write in my diary, using the cartoon on the wall as an aid to memory, my way of inscribing the invisible forces on the world. You would see my mural, and understand what I felt.

As we stood at the glass door that first night you visited, I searched my bag for the key and noticed the dark car pass slowly by. We were being watched. My mother would say, when we were walking down the street, *Someone is keeping an eye on us, little B.*, and at first I thought she meant God, but then I came to understand that it was the voluntary network of spies, the curious, the gossips seeking fodder. Our two dark figures, bulky in winter coats, were reflected in the glass of the door, and then we were inside and going up the stairs. I double-locked and bolted the door behind us and led the way to the bedroom, switched on the lights. You were not pleased by my creation. You stared at it as if at something diseased. Funny, I said, it's really quite funny, but you didn't hear me. I turned off the light and began to tell a story about a man who had treated me with great cruelty, how he had hurt me, lies, of course, but told with passion and tears, and as I told it, I coaxed you, and in the darkness you set aside your shock and distress. When you left I remembered my mother's words, *Someone is keeping an eye on us, little B.*, and I thought of you going out into the street, eyes in a parked car a block away, notes set down. I wondered why we could not be free. The perfect wife had sent her spies. The police suspected you of something—trafficking in love potions.

Near midnight, the year about to end. A few minutes ago I picked up the phone and called my father. He said it was good of me to think of him. *I've been dreaming about your mother a lot*, he said. His search goes on. He was watching the New Year's Eve festivities of television and assumed I must be doing the same. Or at a party. No, I said, I was just thinking about the past and the future. You were always a wise girl, he said.

After you left my apartment, I looked at the wall where I had drawn and written our history, saw it with your eyes. I knew you would never come back while it was there. On my way home from work one night, I stopped at the hardware store and bought a gallon of paint. It took three coats to cover it, and when it was gone I wished that I had I had a photograph of it, a record of what I had made. For every poem there is another secret poem, my professor of love once said. Each of us has hidden stories. I painted over one of mine.

In the top drawer of my filing cabinet a box of chocolate creams that Sam Pruitt gave me for Christmas, and I have taken them out, set them on the table in front of me. I will celebrate the New Year, by eating one or two.

Two identical chocolate creams, one in each hand. Jenny F. and I are paired, doublegoers. The perfect wife too is my twin. Your book is very clever in the way it blurs the two women, the wife and the mistress so that at the end, we do not know who it is that has been killed off. Your doctor-detective sees a gun lying on a chair and picks it up in his shaking hand, the door opens, a gunshot and as he falls, wounded, he pulls the trigger, but we never know who he has murdered. A post-modern elision, with a little ironic epilogue. Because, perhaps, you don't even now understand who it is you wish to kill, whether the succubus who took you in with lies, who intoxicated you with freedoms, or the perfect wife who brings order and good sense into your life, the respected and respectable.

There is only one woman, one man. That's the kind of thing one writes after midnight while eating chocolate creams and remembering what should be forgotten. I imagine a book that continues where yours leaves off, a book where the doublegoers meet and exchange roles. I might have been the perfect wife. Marriage is abstract and governed by rules, a salvation from the perversities of our individual existence with its detailed and wayward desires. A salvation, and yet with time—deprived, hopeless in the face of the routine—even the perfect wife will become once more manipulative, false, lubricious.

Once upon a time I thought I was out of harm's way. I had chosen a sensible arrangement with a musician, the handsome Lonny. I worked in the archives. He did research for his thesis: *False Relation as an Expressive Device in the Early Music of William Byrd.* We spent time together on weekends. I told myself this was sufficient, though a rebellious voice in my head sometimes called him Loony. Once or twice I let it out, and he sulked, and I swore to behave. It was what life must be, I said, until the day I attended a small performance at the Conservatory. Apart from his studies in musicology, Loony was, he had told me, a member of an early music group, played recorder and sang. Everyone has hobbies.

In this public performance he was singing, he said, told me little else. He was, as it emerged, a male alto, falsettist, an imitation castrato, making that strangest of sounds, girlish, outrageous, and he was here presented in a scene of erotic thrills from a seventeenth century opera by Cavalli—Lonny was Endimion, a half-naked shepherd boy, and opposite him a soprano playing Diana, goddess of the Moon, goddess of chastity, and perform-

168

ing Moony and Loony's duet with many an unchaste wiggle of her perky bottom. Loony in a sort of furry bathing-suit and sheepskin cloak, she in revealing pale blue, both stricken with love, goddess and shepherd, hooting like dickiebirds in heat. A deal of kissing, pretending to kiss, withdrawing from a kiss. Voices, soprano and alto, an endless orgasm. False relation indeed. By the end of the month Moony was in Loony's bed, and I was out. I became the goddess of chastity, perforce. A week later I found an advertisement describing the job I now hold. I knew it was time to move on.

I didn't tell you that, not wanting you to know I had been betrayed.

You gave me gifts sometimes but never bought me clothes, as if you wished to avoid too much domestic intimacy. You tried to set limits, to prove you were not deeply involved. There was no place in your plan of a courtly and pragmatic existence for this; you expected a simple system of tension and release, useful, uncomplicated, and what I offered you was a woman who wrote and drew on the walls a crude account of her power over you (yours over her), huge letters at the top saying EVERYONE LOVES ME. You presented a silver bracelet, a respectful and respectable kind of gift, and I ruined the gift by making it part of the mad comedy we were playing out. You gave me an expensive fountain pen to write my diary, and I used it to inscribe tattoos on your secret skin. We must be careful, you said to me. You looked haunted, and I half expected a dark messenger to come from you and murder me. Yet you came back to me, and back, until, in my absence, you escaped. Now I have the book in which you do me in. Foolish of me to pretend that corpse might be that of your seemly and upright spouse. She has a sense of limit, and in a few more years you will settle into a comfortable boredom with her. The naked bleeding corpse is mine. G. warned me about you. I sent her a letter telling her not the truth but some hint of it. Never trust a respectable man, she wrote back.

At the core of your bland, satisfied, life, I will remain, however many times you murder me on paper, for I am more than words on paper. I have invaded your nerves, the primitive stink-eating monsters of the limbic brain have set free their cravings

169

on me. At the sight of me those lizard whims will stir once more, imagination and hunger taking hands and crying for a death. You gave me a name, and it can't be taken back.

The blank face of the stitchery child sickens me now. I want to be rid of it. Shall I lock these pages away before I go into the storage vaults?

Left them. Once in the vaults, in the cleansed air, gloved in white cotton, I began opening drawers at random, looking at needlework, hooked rugs, knitted socks, some of them old and worn but with unique patterns, an Arran sweater knitted long ago, a very beautiful stitch. Each woman's stitchery was unique, I've read, so that when the body of a drowned fisherman washed ashore, no matter how decayed, how eaten by crabs, the woman could recognize it as her own lost man. Wool outlasts the flesh it warmed. I might have knitted such a garment for you, and sent you out into the river on a winter's night, to be swept away, vanishing in the blizzard, going under, lost. I see you as a boy, a heavy anchor holding the boat steady in the current, a fishing rod in your hand, dreaming of a life to come. You looked to see if you were watched, and if not, brought yourself off by the quick work of one hand, and I was there with you, my hand on your hand.

I closed the last of the drawers and moved on to the library shelves, catalogues, reference works, and the section of cookbooks, regional publications from the Women's Institute, various churches, and the handwritten collections of recipes picked up here and there. I took out the one I saw bought at auction. A bright Saturday in October. Your *belle-mère* announced that we must go to this auction—she had seen quilts and hooked rugs in the listing of goods to be sold—that you would drive us there. I hadn't dared to get in touch with you since the afternoon in your examining-room a week before. It was arranged that I would wait in front of this building. She was there in the front seat, and you avoided meeting my eyes. I wondered if you were afraid of me or only wished to tease me by pretending to be distant, professional, the good doctor who had stanched the flow of my blood. As we drove, the older woman in the seat beside you was telling the slightly daring story about how she got to Rome, though I was to gather later on that there was another, and more disreputable version, but it was a lively tale about a woman whose bravery led her where she might not have gone, becoming secretary and driver to a senior staff officer, travelling not far behind the front as the allied troops moved north through Italy, and in Rome meeting the man who became her husband. Not really her husband, the other story went. I suppose you heard both versions, or perhaps, in your upright way you heard only what she wished you to believe. As I listened to her talk, I stared out the window, where the maples along the road caught the sunlight, brilliant scarlet, the annual show. In the farmyard where the auction was being held, fallen leaves were trampled by the small crowd, but the branches held a thousand more. With an affectation of professional care I examined rugs and quilts, though she and I were both as excited as children by the event and wished to buy for the mere glory of it, and we agreed that she would do the bidding, and I stood back from the small crowd and looked at the stone farmhouse, its fine proportions, the mullioned windows. The old farm life had been lived in that house, days dim and sweet, and after the auction it would be bought and renovated, used as a summer home. The auctioneer's voice sang on. She bought one rug and two quilts, and I folded them carefully and took them back to the car, where you opened the trunk for me, and I placed them in it with care, and while we were away from the crowd I spoke to you. At the front of the crowd our leader was bidding on something, and at first I couldn't see what it was, but it appeared to be a box of worn pots and pans. She took possession of it and brought it back to where I was standing. She took out of it an old three-ring binder and showed me that it was full of recipes, written out by pencil in a very small hand, explaining that we ought to begin a collection of recipe books, and this would be the first, and then suddenly she was saying that she had met a friend in the crowd, and they wished to drive back together. N. will drive you, she said.

I've brought the recipe book with me. I had to promise you, the next day before we left the motel, that I would find an excuse to go to some other doctor, to get myself off your list, but I never did. I could make my jokes about threatening you with exposure, the physician who broke his oath by having one of his patients.

The motel scene in your book: an assignation that goes wrong. He goes to the place for cheap love, but she is not there, the woman who's promised to meet him. Restless, he turns on the TV. And on the screen he sees her, playing out her role in the story, as if it were already written, performed for the camera, concluded. A knock on the door, and he finds himself in the hands of the police, accused of being part of a kidnapping plot, sent there to pick up the money. The woman vanishes, leaves him only bitterness. You grew afraid of me. A man fears the eating of his heart.

Tomato cake. I've never heard of such a thing before, a cake made with a tin of tomato soup, brown sugar and butter. I flip the page to a recipe for mustard pickles. Every year in late August Jenny F. takes a few days off to make her pickles. Once she invited me round to help her or perhaps to observe—I didn't know why I was invited—and when I arrived her thick hair was tied up in a scarf, she wore a soiled loose blouse, grey sweatpants with a yellow stain on the thigh. The air was hot, damp, thick with spice. Bottles of mustard pickle stood inverted on the counter. In the heat of the kitchen Jenny—always so perfect, immaculate, carefully dressed—was sweating, and she wiped her forehead with her sleeve. Her husband was away somewhere, avoiding this sensual disorder. It was like a dream where you find yourself in the midst of an orgy, being urged to join in, yet fearing dissolution. As I walked away down the sidewalk, I wondered if the hot, stinking atmosphere was what you found when you came to me, everything tropic, dissolute, famished.

Marge's recipe for Date Loaf. Ammonia Cookies from Bea's mother. Here and there, little drawings, labelled in a child's large printing. A round face with round eyes and mouth, and large tears falling. Printed underneath: *Dorty when she got the Smacks.* A recipe for gumdrop cake has *Good!* printed beside it in the same childish letters, a large heavy exclamation mark at the end. My fingers in their white gloves turned more pages, and I noticed that the fingertips were blackened from the dust on the old paper. Ought to be carefully cleaned by a paper conservator. I looked at the coded tag, which in its numbers and letters made precise reference to that October afternoon in that farmyard with its log barns.

On another page, a recipe for beef stew. About to flip further on when my eye caught a phrase at the end of the instructions, written in the same hand as the recipe, the pencil perhaps pressing a bit harder. Or did I imagine that? *He hit me again. Said I spilled the whole d___ salt box in it.* I pushed aside the book. *Dorty when she got the Smacks.* My face was hot as if a strong hand had clipped me across the cheek. We had stood together under that tall maple and I had imagined the calm and stability of the old life, but this was one of those isolated farms where there was a lot of hitting. G.'s third husband once punched her in the head. She picked up a tin of peas and broke his nose with it, then she had to drive him to the hospital.

I opened the recipe book again: *Stuffed Pork. Mary's recipe (Jim's favourite.)* On another page: *Raisin Cake (from Jim's mother.)* At the foot of the page two round, schematic children's faces, *Dorty and Me* printed beside them, then scribbled out. Beside all this a long shape with a shoe at the bottom, labelled *Uncle Jim's Wooden Leg.* So she married the wrong man, the one who hit her, instead of Jim, who married Mary, and then they all pretended to be friends. Her husband had a better house, a bigger farm lot, and with the wooden leg, she figured Jim was a poor bet. By the time she figured it out that she was wrong Dorty and Me had been born, and she was stuck out there.

In England, there was a nice man—older than I am, happily divorced, as he put it—who said he'd never known anyone like me, so beautiful, he said, so different from the run of girls. When I told him I couldn't stay in England he said he'd move to Canada; he was an experienced draughtsman, he could get work anywhere.

There has to be a perfect husband in the story. The demon lover and the perfect husband, and who does she choose? The lady or the tiger? The life I missed, the woman with her recipe book in the isolation of a cold farmhouse in winter, waiting for her husband to come back, knock her around. Maybe she married him for his passion, but after you've been slapped a few times, sex isn't much of a consolation any more. I turned more pages. *Strawberry Pie, heard on the radio,* and the next page, *Fish Soup, good for Pike or Pickerel.* And at the foot of the recipe a note. *Got this from Jim's mother. Made it for after his funeral.* So Jim was gone by then, and maybe Dorty and Me grown up and left, and did she still get hit? To fill her evenings, she was making those quilts we bought, and the rug, or maybe that was the generation before. Something her husband's mother had sewn in the silent hours when the snow piled up around the house and barn.

It wasn't easy, to shed my own blood. I'd hatched the plan a week before, and made sure that the knife was close at hand, downstairs in the still unrenovated space where we did cataloguing in those days. I had some cardboard that was my excuse for using the sharp hobby knife. I waited until you were in the building, one of our monthly meetings just over. I had concentrated on drawing your eyes toward me, testing the power of thought, and once or twice I knew you glanced my way, and I looked up, as if by accident, and met your look, but if there was a message in your eyes I could not read it. Before you had a chance to leave the building, I walked down the stairs, set out the cardboard, sliced it and then slashed the scalpel blade across the ring finger of my left hand, a deep cut, and it made me cry out, and I seized a tissue from the box to soak up the blood and rushed up the stairs. Alice, our receptionist in those days, was the first to see me, and perfectly following the script, she screamed, and then there you were, took hold of my hand, asked me sternly how I'd done it, and I said the knife had slipped, and in a second, you had taken out a clean white handkerchief, wrapped it round the finger, told me to hold it tightly in my other fist, and we were in your car on the way to the hospital. The finger was throbbing, but I could have cried out, not with pain but with joy. I was in your control, and you were in mine. You had touched me. You would look after me. Another few steps in my arrangements, and you would be mine. *I have plans for you*, the villainess says in your thriller. *The plot is carefully constructed.* Yes, you were right, I had a future in mind for you, and at the hospital, as you cleansed the wound, closed it with sutures, your skin touching mine, your careful stitches closing the gaping hole in my flesh, I was in the first stages of my ecstasy. You were too polite to tell me how stupid I was to cut myself.

As I reach out to turn another page of the cookbook, my finger is throbbing with the pain of that old wound. I can feel your sutures in the healed flesh, almost perfect, with only a tiny scar at one end. You did a good job. You always did a good job. Turn a page. Loose clippings, mostly recipes, fragments of advertisements on the back, Coming Events, a card party. One of the fragments of newsprint, unfolded, proves not to be a recipe, but a short account of the execution of a woman in Louisiana who was convicted of killing her husband and hiding his body in an old well. *Faits divers*, they call such things, the subject matter of the great Russian novels. Her fantasy of escape.

One of my *faits divers*, the short news items of my life: Professor C., who flirted with me after class, and once took me out for a drink, driving us miles away where he thought no-one could recognize us. He never touched me, but flattered me on the subject of my beautiful eyes, my intelligence, stared at me with plaintive devotion, then later gave me a very low mark on my second essay, left it in a box outside his door at the end of the term, when I couldn't find him to complain. That's his little pathetic kind of fuck, G. said when I phoned and told her. I could have murdered him and stuffed him down a well. Hidden bodies—where we stood in the farmyard, perhaps there was a grave beneath our feet. He had found the clipping. I didn't hear her ghost crying out. I could think only of you.

If there are other riddles in the recipe book, I'll leave them there. I suppose it was her only privacy, the only place he wouldn't find what she had concealed, and what's there is elliptical enough, though any husband would see the point of that newspaper story. I could come back to this in daylight, write an essay about the recipe book as an abortive, secret diary. As context, I could discuss the other recipe books in our collection, the way they express a sense of community, ways of cooking passed from hand to hand, the books as a locus of both community and solitude. We have talked about publishing a series of essays on various aspects of the collection, this could be one of them. A little book of such explorations: it will be my secret answer to your secret novel. Your *belle-mère*'s collection has become my playground, my prison. I visited her in hospital, near the end, hoping to find words to express how she had altered my life, drawing me out of my pleasant, unremarkable job in the university archive and bringing me here to this eccentric, factitious assembly of junk, which perhaps made sense only to her. She brought me here, and that afternoon I stared at her pale face in the hospital bed to see whether, on the margin of oblivion, she would tell me the secret, why she had chosen me. *N. has been here to see me*, she said to me, *and I feel the better for it.* Your name was the first word out of her mouth, and there was adoration in her lips' caress of that familiar sound. You had come and gone, avoiding me, afraid perhaps that I had some new trick to take you in.

I was your last appointment in the afternoon, just a few moments to have the stitches you had put in my finger removed, but I insisted on telling you my sad story, so well researched and prepared—the sad tale of my sad tail—my eyes holding yours, pleading for your help, refusing to let you send me to someone else, then pulling the johnnie-shirt all the way up to my waist, feet in the stirrups, your eyes wide, your lips parted. I was unfair.

Dutiful, you had come to the deathbed of your *belle-mère*, some kind of farewell. She had arranged your perfect marriage. She let you go. No sign of her in your novel. You set her free. It comes to me to think that she was the only one you truly loved. I didn't expect love, though I thought I might achieve recognition in your eyes—the osprey at a height, knowing its prey. I told you that only you could release the stricture, ease the pain—lies, but a metaphor for truth. You were the incubus meant to descend on my sleep. Meaning: Oh cutie, I had the hots for you like nobody else.

Was it the wooden leg that kept her from marrying Uncle Jim? She couldn't imagine him taking it off and hopping one-legged into her bed. A one-legged man with an erection would be a rum sight. If I am to write my essay I must avoid such ridiculous speculations.

I will mail this, and you will read it. Or not. Morning will come, and I will walk along the snow-covered streets, leaving the tracks of my shapely little boots in the new snow. I will turn the key in the door of my apartment, and the deadbolt will slide out of its hole. It will be no surprise to find you there, standing naked at the window where you have been watching the street, waiting for my approach. You will turn toward me, and I will be unprepared for a man with no face.

A few weeks ago I arrived home late one dark evening, aware that a car was parked near the door that leads to my apartment, and as I was about to enter, the door of the car opened. I stopped breathing, closed my eyes, my heart beat faster. You had come back.

No.

It was Jenny F.'s husband. She was out of town for a day or so, a family matter she had said to me, carefully not explaining. Perhaps you had summoned her. So here he was, waiting in the dark. As he dressed he asked if he might come back, and I said No. He wrote me a letter which I have saved. It was a day or so later that when I came home to my apartment and knew you had been there, your secret visits beginning once more.

Out there in the winter darkness, your little boat is waiting. It waits for one who will make her escape over the blackness of the frigid water, ice just beginning to form in the shallows. The flight of the imprisoned queen—Mary Queen of Scots, her nineteen years in captivity, and the busy work of her needle. I once had a plan for a book, to be called *The Queen's Needle* and to contain illustrations of all her embroidery panels, signed MS for Mary Stuart, the products of the patient hours of those lost years, her fingers busied while the mind, as quick and tenacious, planned for her escape. Then the assassination of her cold scheming cousin, and at last, the throne of England. This time she would not be distracted by a tall pretty boy, *the lustiest and best-proportioned long man* she had ever set her eyes on. Long, yes, she thought, he would be long, long, long, but in the event, one can guess, what length there was gave little pleasure, and besides that he was a sot, so she took to her bed the Earl of Bothwell. Between the fanatic Covenanters and her chilly cousin, she was trapped. Thus the imprisoned years of needlework and letters and plots, demanding to see the cousin queen she would never meet, and at last, on a cold February morning her head, in its auburn wig, was hacked off. The snow, and the darkness and the waiting boat, the flight she never made, the needlewoman queen, with her habit of ordering the murder of those who inconvenienced her. Fitting the world to the ancient and abstract pattern of her stitchery misled her into the belief that any action she performed would be blessed. It was her cousin who knew with how much caution a woman must proceed, who kept her throne and died in her bed. Whether by luck or tactic Elizabeth was cold, and her virginity was negotiable. When it became necessary, she signed the death warrants.

Who set the trap? Who sprang it? It's possible that my plotting was like that of Mary Stuart, busy and futile. The obfuscating, delaying, indecisive cousin won out. I sit here in the first hours of the new year, telling my story to you, who already know it as another and different story, yours. Perhaps I am not the spider spinning but the web being spun, the creation, not the creator, and I have a sudden vertiginous moment of helplessness, unable to breathe, as if all the complex inner occupations of the body, the soft systems of flow and return, declared their power, their triumph over me. The events of the committee meeting, when I was for the first time interviewed; I wore a suit with a small black and grey check, and a pale grey sweater, tight enough to outline the lovely shape of my breasts, but not tight enough to appear cheap—women must be so careful—and you sat on the far side of the table, affecting to be reticent, untouchable, all the while planning the enticement, a second's glance stripping me naked as you were plotting to have me—meek, helpless. You read on my face my willingness. Had the *belle-mère* brought me to you as a rat is thrown to a caged eagle? The cup of coffee she put in my hand contained the love-potion. She had lost you, but she could continue the enthrallment through me. It was my heart that was to be eaten.

Prisoners. We are all held captive, Mary Stuart in an English castle, her cousin in her masque of royalty. The detective solves only the crime that has been presented for him to solve. That is what books and movies and TV shows are all about, the illusion of meaning. In truth there are many answers to any good question. *Who killed Cock Robin?* The whole of creation.

Not my words: there is no such category in this archive. I am taking the dictation of some night voice invading from the past or the future. And something in the dark brain insists it is my mother's voice, even though I have no memory of any such dark sayings from her. Of course I was a child, and understood as a child, and she would never have told me her most serious thoughts. If she spoke about the universe, she would not have directed the words to the understanding of little B. Our parents fail us in this way, by keeping us safe from the vertiginous complexity of their most wonderful thoughts. My job is not to enlarge the range of speculation, but to create order, to place what has gone before in clear and consistent categories so that access to all we've saved is easy. I am an archivist. I clear the path to the desired information.

Morning is coming toward us across the world, the bland sanity of daylight into which you will vanish like all my memories. On top of my filing cabinet in a wooden tray is a letter from a large textile museum asking about material they are seeking for a planned exhibition. I might turn my chair to the computer keyboard and draft an answer. I have already sorted through the catalogue and made a list of possibilities.

Though it is early and still dark, the lacemaker is already at work, and her time is not the time of a clock but is measured out by her quick needle as it draws the thread over and over again, ten stitches, a hundred, a thousand, an inch of work accomplished, an eternity of wasted life to produce the flounce of a wide collar. As worn by Voltaire, Pompadour, the King himself. She bends toward the candle to see that each detail is perfect. Back and forth, her needle takes control of the air. In the previous century she mastered embroidery. In a future century she will learn knitting. When I go home I will attend to my household duties, sleep, perhaps phone G. later in the day. I won't talk for long. I sense that the newest husband resents my calls, especially if we fall into old joking ways and start to giggle. He is younger than she is, and very handsome, G. says. I have never seen him.

I might put on the white gloves, turn more pages of the recipe book, searching out the clues, but you would not care to hear them. You have your own stories to tell, the adventures of your doctor-detective, the villainess who appears, unexpectedly, wherever he goes, a figure in the hospital corridor, or at the health club where he works out, a woman in grey sweats lifting weights and then appearing at the pool, a naked figure blurred by the plastic goggles he wears. He wonders what it is she wants from him. To lead him to destruction, an assignation at a cheap motel where the police arrest him, and later, when he seeks her apartment, he is struck on the head, knocked unconscious. The Nervous System that chapter is called. She is the embodiment of arcane knowledge, what must not be revealed. It was clever of you to have Jenny F. give me that book, to taunt me with your triumph.

I returned the recipe book to its place on the shelves. To write about it, I would need to search all the other handwritten collections to see if they have stories to tell, a few mysteries, clippings about whales beaching themselves on a distant island, a soldier appearing out of the jungle, a woman who left her fortune to a bird. The Nervous System. I looked about me as I stood in front of the bookshelves, cases of stored material on all sides, and it no longer cried out to be seen.

We are going through the woods, and it is spring, and you lay me down on the wet ground with the mud and roots, open me slowly like one of the buds on the tree above us, everything damp and swollen with the annual germination. I can no more resist you than the earth can resist the lengthening light. I have invented you for this moment. I will go away, and when I return your absence will be all I know. I can write no more of this. Time to fold it up and put it in its envelope. Soon it will be daylight, and I will set the alarms for the building, slip on my dark overcoat, wrap the white cashmere scarf around my neck and set out to walk to my apartment, the footsteps of my little boots in the snow behind me, a trail easy to follow for anyone who might wish to track me. The January sunlight, reflected from the white crystalline surface of the snow, will be bright. As I walk through it I am scandalously beautiful.

ELISABETH HARVOR won the Malahat Novella Prize in 2004 for "Across Some Dark Avenue of Plot He Carried Her Body." The story was also a finalist for a National Magazine Award in the spring of 2005. Her latest novel, *All Times Have Been Modern*, has just been released in paperback.

KRISTA BRIDGE has appeared in the *Toronto Life* Summer Fiction issue, *Prism international* and *Prairie Fire*, and has been nominated for a National Magazine Award. A collection of short stories, *The Virgin Spy*, is forthcoming in the spring of 2006. "A Matter of Firsts" will also be included in the *Journey Prize Anthology*.

DARRYL WHETTER has published fiction in *The New Quarterly, broken pencil* and *The Fiddlehead,* and criticism in the *Globe and Mail* and *National Post*. His first collection of stories, *A Sharp Tooth in the Fur*, was released in 2003 and selected to the *Globe and Mail* list of 100 Recommended Books. His essays and interviews have been published in France, Germany, Canada, the United States and India.

DAVID WHITTON lives in Toronto. His fiction has appeared in *The Dalhousie Review*, *The New Quarterly* and *Taddle Creek*. He is currently working on a first collection of short stories.

MICHAEL BRYSON is the author of *Thirteen Shades of Black and White* and *Only a Lower Paradise*. He is also the founder and editor of the online literary journal *The Danforth Review*. He lives in Toronto, and works for the Ontario government.

VIVETTE J. KADY grew up in South Africa and now lives in Toronto. Her fiction has appeared in numerous journals and anthologies in Canada and the United States, including the *Journey Prize Anthology*, *Coming Attractions* and *Best Canadian Stories*, and has been shortlisted for the Journey Prize, a National Magazine Award and a Western Magazine Award. A collection of stories, *Most Wanted*, was published in 2005.

ELISE LEVINE is the author of the short-story collection *Driving Men Mad* and the novel *Requests and Dedications*. Her work has appeared in *Coming Attractions*, the *Journey Prize Anthology* and the *National Post*, among other publications. Originally from Toronto, she currently lives in Chicago.

KIM AUBREY was born and raised in Bermuda, but has spent the better part of her life in Toronto. Her stories have appeared in *Event*, *Pagitica*, *The Berkshire Review* and *Upstreet*, and have been nominated for the Journey Prize and a Pushcart Prize. Her essays have been published in *The Literary Review of Canada*, *North Dakota Quarterly* and *The Writer's Chronicle*.

DAVID HELWIG was born in Toronto, lived for many years in Kingston and now lives in Prince Edward Island. He is the author of many books of poetry and fiction, and was a founder of Oberon's *Best Canadian Stories*. *The Year One*, a book-length poem, won the 2004 Atlantic Poetry Prize.

DOUGLAS GLOVER is the author of four story collections and four novels, including the critically acclaimed *The Life and Times of Captain N*, as well as a collection of essays, *Notes Home from a Prodigal Son*. His stories have been reprinted in *Best American Short Stories*, *Best Canadian Stories* and *The New Oxford Book of Canadian Stories*, and his criticism has appeared in the *Globe and Mail*, *New York Times Book Review*, *Washington Post Book World* and *Los Angeles Times*. He has been the editor of *Best Canadian Stories* since 1996. His most recent novel, *Elle*, won the Governor General's Award for Fiction in 2003. A collection of critical essays on Glover's work edited by Bruce Stone, *The Art of Desire*, appeared in 2004.